Kira and Cassandra

Selected Reviews of David Osborn's Previous Novels

The Last Pope

"A truly great novel. I plan to make it my finest motion picture."

—Martin Poll, producer of *The Lion in Winter,* starring Peter O'Toole and Katharine Hepburn

"A thrilling blend of history, religion, and human relationships."

—*The New York Post*

The Glass Tower

"Breathless introduction to the inner workings of big business …"

—*The Times* Literary Supplement

"[An] institution story perfected by Zola and none the worse for it … deftly, excitingly told."

—*The Daily Telegraph*

"A sharp and entertaining first from Mr. Osborn, who is already an accomplished screenwriter."

—*Lincolnshire Evening Telegraph*

Murder on Martha's Vineyard

"A good tale of mystery and murder. Its plot twists and turns in and out of an intriguing whodunit that packs a punch at the end powerful enough to floor one."

—*Western Morning News*

"This is the first entry in what might become a promising new series.… Osborn has created an interesting protagonist."

—*Publishers Weekly*

Murder on the Chesapeake

"Satisfying tale … intrepid sleuth."

—*Publishers Weekly*

"The tale is spun tightly and the main characters are engaging."

—*Chicago Sun Times*

Open Season

"A truly brilliant novel … an accomplished writer in all media, but ultimately a pro … a superbly organized book, brutal, chilling, but carrying a terrible conviction."

—*Canberra Times*

"This well-plotted thriller makes compulsive holiday reading."

—*Salisbury Journal*

Kira & Cassandra

David Osborn

Published by Dagmar Miura
Los Angeles
www.dagmarmiura.com

Kira and Cassandra

First published 2024

ISBN: 979-8-89195-027-6

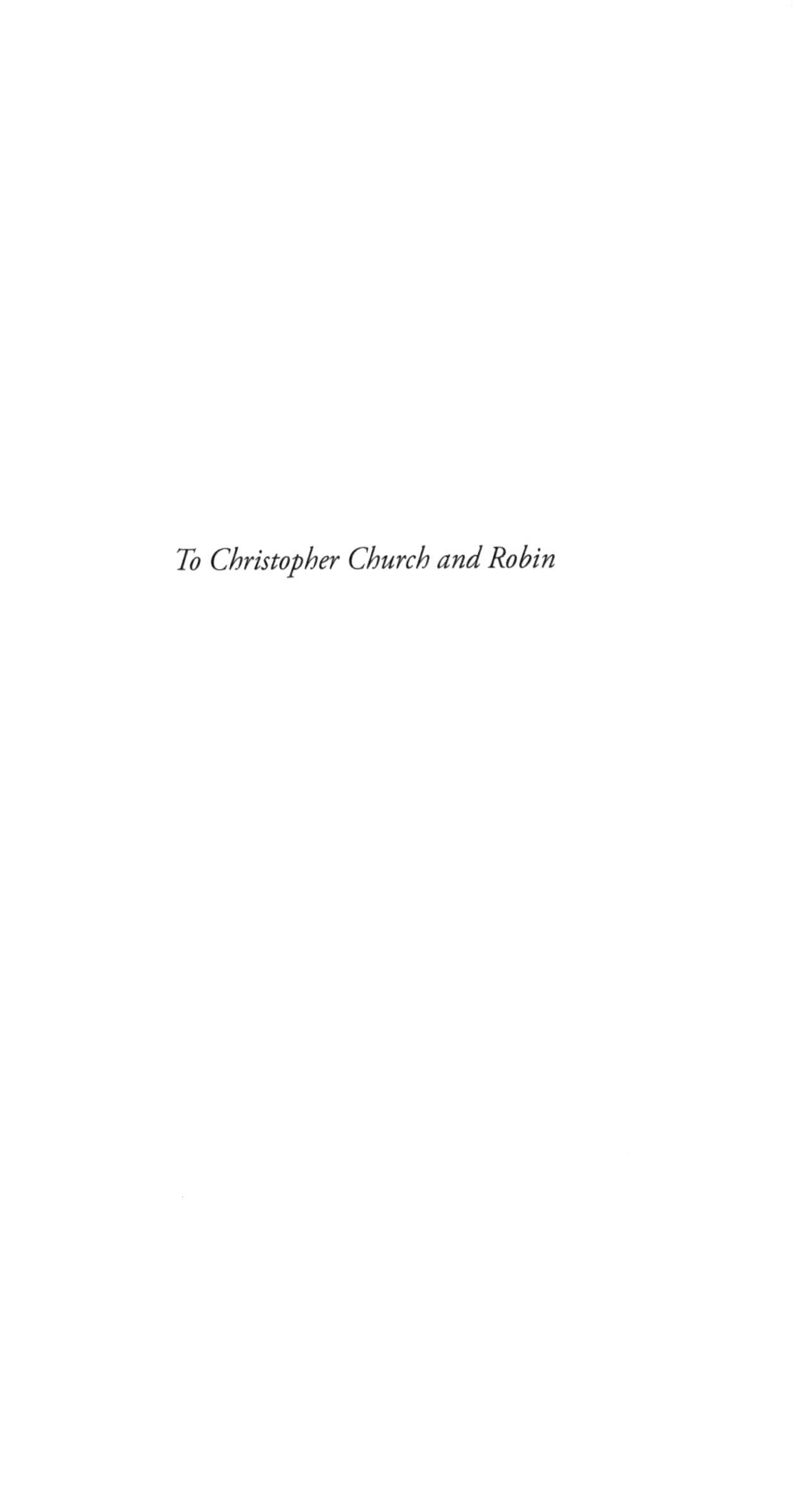

To Christopher Church and Robin

One

The bell high in the tower of the old church tolled a mournful end to the funeral of the Reverend Andrew Pollack, better known to the large number of mourners as simply Father Andrew. Before death finally took him, the deeply loved benign old Catholic priest had presided over the Eucharist and mass at St. Mary Magdelene, which for some fifty years, along with its graveyard, lay like an island of peace on the outskirts of the busy city.

Those mourners still remaining at prayer by the graveside and braving a cold drizzle, as well as others who slowly left, reflected the general poverty of the community in the city to which the venerable old church belonged. Both the clothing and manner of many told of the working-class, and the often-seen blond hair indicated that some were descendants of immigrants from Northern European countries such as Lithuania and Latvia, bordering on Sweden and the Baltic Sea.

One of those still by the grave was Anna Petruska, a gaunt, weary white-haired woman in her late seventies. A niece of Father Andrews, the daughter of the priest's oldest brother who had also recently passed away, she had served for over forty years as the priest's housekeeper in the rectory close by St. Mary Magdelene, washing his linen, cooking his meals, cleaning the priest's own simple three-room quarters, and living herself in another small room of the rectory.

Heartsick at Father Andrew's passing, Anna finally left the gravesite and made her way amidst the graves, many, like the church, showing the wear of several hundred years. The distance to the rectory was short, but she stopped here and there to catch her beath or simply to rest her legs.

Greeted by silence where once there had been the warm voice of the old priest chatting about his parishioners, Anna sat in in the rectory's stark kitchen, staring into the gathering darkness of late autumn, hearing nothing and seeing only endless memories of the priest who had filled so much of her empty and barren life.

It was not until a brief distant sound of the town's siren announced five o'clock, and the end of the day, did she rise and make herself a cup of tea, and when seated again, it was only when she'd half finished her tea did she find the courage to pick up the envelope from the kitchen table addressed to her by its sender, Father Andrew. She had received it two days earlier, the day the good priest had died, and it had remained unopened because of the instruction on the envelope's back in Father Andrew's shaky scrawl: "Open only when I am gone."

Using a kitchen knife and very carefully opening the envelope, Anna extracted two things. One was a handwritten note to her from Father Andrew that said:

Dearest Anna,

I trust only you to please personally convey the accompanying enclosed letter to Detective Alter Weiss at our local police precinct. Give it to nobody but him, and God bless you and keep you, dearest child.

Yours forever,

Father Andrew

Anna stared at the other letter's blank exterior for a long while, surprised and wondering why the dear old priest had written to such a person as Detective Weiss. It could only be, perhaps, about work she knew they had mutually shared on interfaith community projects, some involving a series of Anti-Defamation League trainings for teachers at the schools of the city. Detective Alter Weiss was Jewish.

The letter Father Andew asked Anna Petruska

to deliver remained on her kitchen table for over a week before Anna summoned courage to take it to Detective Weiss at the 5th Precinct Police Station.

Two

lter Weiss, commonly known to col-
leagues at work as well as friends as
Alt, or just plain Weiss, was a vet-
eran police detective whose intelligence and ded-
ication had over the years seen him rise from the
uniformed ranks to be his precinct's lead detective
in major crime and homicide.

No longer young but far short still of retirement, his work for years had taken him throughout the crowded and often dangerous streets of the
wide city area his precinct encompassed and which
included, along with the old church of St. Mary
Magdelene, the multinational slum area known as
the Baltic Ghetto, overcrowded with Lithuanians,
Latvians, Estonians, and Russians, many of them
relatively recent immigrants who still struggled to

find a footing in their new country.

Alter belonged to a small reformed synagogue and was an officer with a deep social conscious that he shared with his wife, Dana, a clinical psychologist working for the city, and who with him had raised three children, two of whom were still in high school. Influenced by her, Weiss saw being a police officer not so much a way to enforce the law as a way to use the law to help people steer clear from the endless morass of often dangerous antisocial problems in his precinct that frequently led to crime.

As a detective, he had long partnered with a much older veteran officer who had recently taken early retirement due to onrushing macular degeneration that, when already causing him not to see clearly, had nearly cost him his life in a particularly dangerous arrest. Now Weiss struggled to calm the often reckless impulses of a new partner, a young woman named Grace Garrity who had only recently come up from driving a patrol car in uniform to being a detective.

Alter Weiss's day usually began with an early start at eight o'clock and found him at his desk with coffee in the crowded crime division on the police station's second floor, getting rid of endless onerous paperwork before delving into leads in a latest case. It was on such a morning, when he'd first seen his kids off to school, and his wife, Dana, had gone to her social work, that Weiss received a phone call from the desk sergeant downstairs to tell him there was a lady who wanted to see him.

"A lady? What Lady?" Weiss could think of no woman involved in the current case he was pursuing.

There were muffled sounds of the sergeant talking to someone, and then she came back with, "Says her name is Anna Petruska and that she has a letter from Father Andrew. She says the priest had told her to deliver it to nobody but you."

Father Andrew? Weiss had worked intimately with the Catholic priest on one case after another affecting parishioners at St. Mary Magdelene, and he and Father Andrew, dismissing any religious differences, had worked closely together and become firm friends.

Weiss had a good memory, but just the same, trying to identify Anna Petruska from somewhere in the back of his mind, took a moment. When he finally recalled her as a niece of his old friend, and his having seen her at the priest's funeral, he told the desk sergeant to send her up.

When she appeared, escorted by a uniformed officer, she turned out to be the same work-worn elderly lady Weiss remembered, and he quickly pulled a chair up close to his desk, politely told her to please be seated, and asked what he could do for her.

She hesitated, looking frightened by where she found herself, amidst the now busy and noisy office scene of officers and plainclothes detectives diving into endless police work. Telephones jangled, men shouted information at each other, with some gathering in knots to review a case or to plan. Twisting her hands in her lap and looking around almost furtively as though breaking some rigid rule, Anna at first was unable to speak. Weiss waited. He was used to people being anxiously silent when at his desk, regardless of the reason, and when finding themselves in a police station, whether upstairs with the detectives or downstairs talking to the desk sergeant and surrounded by uniformed cops.

When Anna finally broke the silence in her heavily accented English, she first stumblingly revealed who she was, that she had come to see him at the request of her uncle, Father Andrew, and to bring to him, and to no one else, a letter contained in one she had received only the day the priest had died. Then, fumbling in her handbag, she produced the letter she'd received with the priest's scrawled instructions to bring to Weiss the enclosed unopened envelope on which was written in shaky scrawled letters, "For Detective Weiss only."

Taking the envelope from her, something told Weiss not to open it there. "Thank you," he said. "I shall be glad to honor Father Andrew's request. I won't show what he's written to anyone."

With that, he slipped the envelope into the safety of the inside breast pocket of his jacket, thanked Anna, saying he was sure Father Andew, unquestionably in heaven, would be silently grateful for her respecting his wishes, and gave Anna his card, telling her to call any time she wished.

Then, and rising from his desk, he summoned the uniform who had showed her upstairs from the sergeant's desk and asked the man to please see Ms. Petruska out and also to see that she was driven home if she wished.

Slightly surprised at such a display of courtesy to so obviously an unimportant person, the uniformed officer obeyed, and Anna Petruska, a little less frightened by her surroundings, was gone with a sense of relief that she had fulfilled Father Andrew's wishes.

Three

Grace Garrity saw to it that Detective Alter Weiss didn't have time even to think about the letter from Father Andrew concealed safely in the inner breast pocket of his jacket. His new partner virtually and without a "Good morning" threw herself at him in a chair by his desk in a sudden excited appearance.

"Guess what!"

Guess what turned out to be a vital telephone clue she had uncovered after hours of meticulously studying phone records in their investigation of the chief suspect in a late-night armed robbery of a convenience store in which the clerk had been shot and severely injured. That in turn galvanized into wakeful action a slightly unwilling Alter Weiss, just beginning his second Styrofoam cup of office coffee and into total forgetfulness of Father Andrew's letter.

And in the long day's flurry of action ending with an arrest, which Weiss grudgingly attributed to Garrity, the letter remained forgotten in his pocket until he took off the jacket on arriving at his small suburban home too late for dinner and only in time to wish his children good night and apologize to his wife, Dana, for his lateness, when she didn't need any apology for work interference in their personal life.

"What's important," she said, "is not dinner, but that you nailed the bastard. That's what's important."

She was like that, always patiently understanding of the endless disruption in their family life caused by his relentless work. Crime never ceased to end, and she herself often had a part in coping with its beginnings in the too often family disputes she found herself settling in her work as a clinical psychologist.

"Garrity did the nailing, actually," Weiss said.

Dana laughed. "And you hate to admit it. Never mind; she'll grow up fast on the job. From what I understand, they all do."

Alter had shed his jacket onto the couch, and she'd started to hang it on the back of a chair, when the envelope he'd slipped into its inside breast pocket fell to the floor. She held it out to him. "Need this?"

And the detective suddenly remembered the

letter, which he had completely forgotten, and the appearance at his desk of the frail visitor and her broken English.

"Damn. Forgot all about it. It's a letter from Father Andrew that was hand-delivered to me early this morning."

"The priest?" The name caught Dana by surprise.

"Yeah, the one I often worked with. Lovely old guy. Wrote it just before he died, apparently."

Alter opened the sealed envelope to extract two folded pages, which he scanned at first quickly just to get the gist of what was written, but then, while his wife waited, seeing him look slightly askance, patiently reading again, and very slowly, a long message in the shaky handwriting of the very old, with other signs of age in missing words and misspellings.

When finished, Alter looked up at his wife and said, "You're the psychologist of the family. I think you should read this."

She took the letter, and just as her husband had done, first scanned it quickly, then, surprised, read it slowly and carefully. When she was finished, and after a moment's silence, in which her expression showed dismay, she said, "My God, Alt. What in the name of heaven are you going to do?"

"Right now, I have absolutely no idea," he replied.

Four

lter Weiss and his wife, Dana, were late that night in getting to bed. Neither spoke of the letter while seeing their children safely asleep, and the letter that had left them both virtually silent was carefully put away in a drawer until they could talk.

"I think it extraordinary that Father Andrew would break his vows of the confessional to write this," Alter said. "No wonder he asked his niece to deliver it personally."

"He clearly must have thought," Dana responded, "that such a serious crime in the eyes of God had been committed that it not just allowed him to break the rules of the confessional but compelled him to."

"But why pick me to tell?" her husband asked.

"Why not some lawyer?"

"Clear enough," Dana answered. "Because he'd worked with you and trusted you and didn't trust anybody else."

She scanned the letter again. "Alt, looking at this from Father Andrew's point of view, this is worse than sin. This is a social enormity, possibly even a serious crime. Practically, and apart from any religious feelings, the revelation of it, if it somehow gets out, could possibly mean screaming lawsuits, to say nothing of heartbreaking and deeply disturbing emotional upheavals. We can only hope that Father Andrew, for all his holiness, hadn't at some time hesitated to reveal what he writes. And if we take any thoughtless action, the Carleson family, and he is clear he means the family of the wealthy state senator who also flaunts an empire of hedge-fund franchises, with all the political clout that gives him, would be ripped apart, and the bloody media would have a field day. What I find astonishing, is *how* the woman did it. I mean for God's sake, Alt, swapping her baby for the Carleson child practically right under the Carleson mother's nose!"

Alter said, "I guess regularly coming to their household for cleaning, she knew their habits. When their baby would be left alone. And besides, it most likely wasn't the child's mother looking after the Carleson child but a nanny, who was probably taking a break while it slept."

"And all the time nobody apparently ever

noticing the cleaning woman's pregnancy?" Dana was incredulous.

"Why would they?" Alter said. "I don't see being pregnant a sign you are plotting to swap your child for somebody else's when it's born. And anyway, since she was just an especially lowly person, hired to do the heavy work that the household servants avoided, such as cleaning toilets and coal-burning ovens and fireplaces, she was probably somebody that nobody paid any attention to. I could hardly tell you anything about the woman who cleans our detective offices. She just comes and she goes. She could change color, become bright green for all I'd know."

After a moment's silence, and scanning the letter again, Dana said, her tone almost awed, "How on earth did she ever manage it? I guess she must have brought her own baby into the house hidden under her skirt or apron, and well-fed and asleep, perhaps as a bundle of cleaning equipment in her cleaning trolley. Did she have help? She must have."

"I don't think so," Alter said, "Other than just her name, Emilija, which is Lithuanian, we know nothing about her except the few things Father Andrew gathered and reveals, which shows that she was desperately poor and more than likely did it alone."

"I don't even want to think of her mental state," Dana said. "With her baby, like the Carleson one, only six weeks old, whatever psychological storm she was in had to be almost unfathomable unless the woman was completely calloused. I mean, exchanging her child for another? Oh, my God, how sick can you get?"

"Yeah, I know," Alter said. "But from rags to riches? It might have been something coldly calculated. The Carlesons are filthy with money, a stable full of horses, that huge yacht, homes in Europe and the Caribbean as well as here. She could have said, Why can't my child have all of that too? And have had her mind pretty well made up beforehand to see that her child did."

Weiss managed a wry half-humorous smile. "We'll never know. But here's a thought. Maybe it's just the cop in me, but did you ever think that the swapped Carleson child might have been an idiot, and it was all arranged for a fee?"

Dana wasn't amused. "Stop it, Alt. Poor Father Andrew wouldn't have fallen for that. It was a confession he heard, remember? And one he carried around in his heart for how many years, does it say?"

"Fifteen," her husband replied, checking down through the letter. "And one apparently made when both children were around ten or eleven years old. Which means that today, the Carleson child must be what? Something around twenty-five? And never knowing all her growing-up years, when wealthy and rich as hell, that whatever her real name was, it was not Cassandra."

"And it's not just the Carleson child facing that she's not who she thinks she is," his wife said. "If she ever has to. Think about the other child also learning who she actually was. It would almost surely be deeply disturbing to either one."

Both she and her husband were silent a moment until the detective said, "Yeah, right. But speculating aside, why do you think Father Andrew wanted me to know about all the sick horror of this that he as a priest felt he couldn't keep to himself? Or even if he thought intelligently about it. Unless we don't have the whole story, and that means knowing more about both a mother named Emilija-something and the child she stole from its wealthy crib.

"We know what became of the life of the cleaning woman's own child become a Carleson. Private schools, horses, dogs, sailboats, and an heiress to millions. I'll have Garrity check that out with some excuse or other.

"But what about the other child, the one born to all those riches only to be involuntarily removed? Whatever happened to her? Did she become a drug addict, a hooker, or even a cleaning woman for life, like the mother who had stolen her? Any one of those lives are possible in the quarter into which she was probably dragged and raised. My guess is that would be what we call the Baltic Ghetto.

"And knowing what happened to her," Weiss continued, "is, I think, precisely why Father Anrew revealed what that poor cleaning woman confessed to. I suspect he was always desperately worried over the stolen child's fate."

"You're right, Alt," Dana said. "But you're a cop, and unless you decide to simply forget about it, you could perhaps find out better than anyone."

In the morning, detective Alter Weiss put Father Andrew's letter to him, revealing what he had heard in the confessional at St. Mary Magdelene, in his and his wife's home safe.

Five

Alter Weiss knew nothing of the cleaning woman named Emilija who Father Andrew said had confessed to exchanging her baby for the Carleson child, and realizing he would need to learn something about her in order to find out what had happened to the child she'd stolen, the detective started a search at St. Mary Magdelene's for who she was. Visiting the ancient church, he collared the church's janitor, whom he had once used as a witness in a vandalism case. But he learned only that the woman had often come to the church, especially on cold nights, to huddle silently in an unused pew, nodding off to sleep in the warmth.

"She rarely spoke to anyone," the janitor said, explaining that when she did, her English was broken and heavily accented. She seemed desperately poor, he went on to tell Weiss, and looked old beyond her years with beginning signs of white hair and a lined face. She came in worn work clothes that never changed and in the few years he'd observed her, she was always cloaked in the same old threadbare cloth coat.

Did she still brazenly work for the Carlesons, the detective wondered? It seemed unlikely. And if not, where was she working now? Or perhaps not working at all. For that matter, was she even living? She could have died of cancer or in an accident. Life expectancy in the Baltic Ghetto slum, where Alter Weiss figured she lived, was lower than in most places.

And most of all, had she even continued as the stolen Carleson's baby's mother, or had she possibly abandoned it? There were legal issues here too, the detective realized. In his need for utmost discretion, Weiss for a start depended on well-known public knowledge. The stolen Carleson child was Carleson's only heir other than his wife, Rowena, a notoriously frivolous woman. A DNA test, if for any doubtful reason one would be taken, could reveal the child who he and his wife were raising wasn't theirs.

Or, Weiss thought, adding one more complexity to his search, what if word of what the cleaning woman had done had somehow leaked out to someone who had decided to use blackmail to extort money Carleson could afford to pay in order to avoid a scandal that might find his financial affairs investigated?

He summoned Grace Garrity. And when his new partner appeared, eager to please and get along, he said, "Grace, got a job for you. I want a profile of Arthur Carleson's family, especially his daughter Cassandra."

Grace looked startled. "Gosh, chief. Do you mean *the* Arthur Carleson?"

"The hedge fund billionaire state senator? Yes. And because of who he is and the political clout he exercises, even over you and me, probably, you're to use, needless to say, complete discretion. Do your search outside your regular work and speak to no one about what you find, especially on Carleson's daughter, who I understand is in her mid-twenties and quite a well-known activist with the UWW, that's the United World Women outfit. Take your time, no rush, and tell no one. Prepare a full report to me on it."

Leaving a mystified but eager-to-please Grace to get on with it, Detective Weiss turned his attention back to the cleaning woman who Father Andrew's confession said had kidnapped the Carleson child, replacing it with her own baby.

Weiss had early on realized even while still discussing the priest's letter with his wife that finding the cleaning woman with only the Lithuanian name Emilija to go on wasn't going to be easy. She probably never paid taxes or registered for voting, and as was often the case with many desperately poor immigrant workers, she might not even be registered with any known employment agency.

But just the same, agencies were a good place to start, Weiss thought after finding nothing on her in police records. He made a list of agencies that sought jobs for cleaning ladies and to which he thought the woman described by the church janitor might have applied, choosing those in poorer sections as ones the woman would have been more likely to go to, rather than those catering more to the wealthy.

He drew a blank with the first four agencies he contacted. "Emilija who? Never had anybody called that. And who knows if that was her real name. Never can tell with some of these immigrants. They lie more than they tell the truth."

But persistence paid off, and Weiss finally achieved success with a small and insignificant employment agency that went by the name of Your Job Inc.

Although it seemed hardly one that would connect in any way with such a wealthy client as the Carlesons, he paid an unannounced visit to the agency's second-floor walk-up that looked down on a street notorious for its petty criminal activities, and the proprietor of which was one Anatole Velinsky, whose appearance matched his doubtful surroundings.

Street-wise Weiss knew at once that the overweight Velinsky, whose pale, slightly bulging-eyed, ever-shifting look never met his own, had a number of things going for him that had nothing to do with finding employment for cleaning ladies. Your Job Inc., which he knew at once from long experience, was a legitimate legal front for illicit pool hall gambling, a hooker protection racket, and a host of other unsavory criminal activities.

There'd be a case here for Grace, Weiss thought, even while eventually extracting information from long unopened files that a woman by the name of Emilija had for nearly a dozen years been sent out to apply herself for jobs at a number of small businesses as well as to private residences in a far wealthier section of town. The agency had done nothing more than t supply women looking for work with the names of employers known to be seeking help. Velinsky had given a list that contained the Carlesons among many to the Emilija woman, but for the past twenty years, the agency had heard nothing from her and so had crossed her off its books.

The woman's surname? Weiss held his breath while Velinsky took what seemed forever to thumb through an old ledger book of appointments before finally coming up with it. It was Paulauskas, and Weiss felt as though he'd hit lucky at roulette.

He added things up. It might make sense, he thought, to presume Emilija Paulauskas was either dead or gone elsewhere, but given Father Andrew's confession as being one the priest had heard over twenty years ago, the presumption of death was almost surely right. The cleaning lady would hardly have moved to another city or even to a different part of the police precinct that was served by the church of St. Mary Magdelene. So, Weiss thought, perhaps it would be smart to check city death notices first, then birth registrations. In short, when had the cleaning woman died, and especially when she'd given birth to a baby she'd swapped for another, and, if possible, what her own real baby's name might have been?

Weiss wrote down the names and addresses of each of those places the Lithuanian lady was given by Your Job Inc. to clean and left with a silent promise to himself that Anatole Velinsky would soon be visited by police detective Grace Garrity.

Six

When winter's icy winds sifted harshly through the narrow streets of the crowded Baltic Ghetto slum, there was little if any heat in the tiny walk-up two rooms that long before police detective Weiss's investigation was home to Lithuanian immigrant Emilija Paulauskas and her daughter. Emilija often found refuge at St. Mary Magdelene from the bitter cold, where she'd sit silently asleep in a pew enveloped in blessed warmth and virtually unnoticed even on days when the priest was celebrating mass or the Eucharist and the pews were filled with people.

Clutching first a six-week-old baby daughter wrapped in several blankets and held closely hidden next to the warmth of her body, sometimes secretly nursing her, she would sit silently until the baby grew first into childhood, then entered school, and she came to the refuge of the church without her. And throughout those early years, she suffered an increasingly burdensome guilt, which, only an occasional vague flickering in her first days of instinctively mothering the child, became an ever increasing torment that seemed everywhere within her, leaving room for little else.

Until one day the guilt became unbearable, and she had sought to rid herself of it in the protective darkness of the confessional, where after first stumbling words of initial hesitation she had poured out all the agony she lived with to Father Andrew.

Forced by the vows of the confessional into shocked silence, the priest listened numbly to how the Lithuanian woman had taken the Carleson infant Cassandra from her crib, leaving her own infant in her place. In the damp cold silence, his head bent close to the lattice separating him from the tortured confessor, the old priest heard in stumbling heavily accented words, first of the untimely death of the woman's husband, which had left her with a late in life pregnancy and with no support, then how, after all her wearying anxious months of pregnancy, and all the pain and terror of being alone with birth when finally her swollen body was free of the burden of pregnancy and with the strangeness of a newborn pressed against her breast, she was very soon back at work.

It was in the large kitchen of the wealthy Carleson home, Emilija confessed, that she suddenly found herself imagining her child, hidden away for the brief time she worked in the salvaged stroller she'd made into a cleaning-equipment trolley, as having the same wealth and privilege as the child she knew was born to the Carleson woman almost at the same time as her own but in a hospital where there were doctors and nurses to help.

And then slowly, but more and more often, that imagination turned into a burning desire to see it happen, a ferocious and obsessive belief that such wealth was her own child's absolute right and that the child born to the wealthy Carleson woman was a usurper who had no such right.

Even today, she told the priest almost eleven years later, that at night when alone she worried endlessly about the safety of Kira, her grandmother's name she'd given the Carleson's child. Kira, whom she'd dared to hope she could give a good life, was instead always out in the streets amidst her gang of young girls, led by Masha, an older and lawless Russian girl, all thinking as they headed into a night of troublemaking that they had the world at their feet.

How very carefully she'd planned it all. Neither her baby nor the Carleson child named Cassandra were large when not yet two months old. They looked enough alike that only a mother could tell the difference, and Mrs. Carleson, suffering postpartum depression, had turned Cassandra over to a strictly trained English nanny whose main interest was in keeping the baby to a rigid schedule and her nursery in perfect order.

How very carefully too she had picked the moment for stealing away Cassandra when she knew the infant, like her own Kira, would be fed and quietly asleep.

How very carefully she had dressed her own baby in the same expensive clothes as the Carleson baby and which she had found on nursery shelving and then had dressed her Kira with before hiding Kira in a bundle of cleaning rags and cleaning equipment in her battered trolley.

And how quickly she had managed the exchange at just the right moment when the nanny was out of the nursery having coffee in the kitchen.

There'd been not a murmur from either child while she'd held her breath in terror as she took the Carleson child, Cassandra, from her crib, as she'd planned and imagined a hundred times, quickly wrapping her in disguising rags and secreting her in the trolley, then putting her own baby, Kira, in her place.

In a flash, and after telling a servant that her cleaning work was finished, she was gone from the Carleson home, and Cassandra had become Kira, and Kira had taken place in the Carleson home as Cassandra.

But over the years, Emilija's work cleaning became harder and harder as deadly arthritis began crippling her hands and knees, making it increasingly difficult to manage even the simplest task, until one day at one house and after spilling fireplace ashes everywhere, her age was finally noticed, and she was coldly told that her services were no longer needed.

It was the first of several such offhanded dismissals and Emilija told the priest how, when struggling home one night through a cold drizzling rain, she finally had accepted that her work days were over, and in hopeless despair wondered how could she keep a roof over hers and her daughter's heads. What would happen to them both? Kira, for many years no longer Cassandra, was soon to become a woman, her eleventh birthday still six months away, and was too young to work. Any thought of the future had suddenly become one of fear and darkness.

Seven

Leaving the confessional that inevitable day and praying for strength and some sign of hope, Emilija stumbled from the safety of St. Mary Magdelene to finally reach her two rooms, where she found Kira just leaving.

"Meeting friends," Kira threw out casually as she left their rooms, refusing Emilija's demand she stay at home and laughing at Emilija's concerns.

So, Emilija had tea alone, and when it got late went to the bed she shared with Kira, after suffering one more evening of lonely anxiety mixed with anger over Kira's laughing refusal to say more about "meeting friends," which Emilija had learned usually meant if not fighting a boy gang, then joining a party where drugs abounded.

The day she had brought Kira, born Cassandra,

from her wealthy crib to the old wooden crate she had salvaged and fixed as a crib for her very early years, Emilija had unexpectedly felt a growing mother's love for the child, who had responded, more often than not, with the warm affection that most any child felt for its mother. "Mom" came easily and naturally to Kira.

At the same time, she often proved difficult. First as a difficult feeder, often colicky, a difficult sleeper, crying endlessly for no apparent reason, difficult when becoming a toddler and struggling against any sort of necessary restraint, difficult when starting school by hating it and more often than not refusing to go, difficult with tears and anger when she suffered a first change from childhood to womanhood, difficult as she became endlessly influenced by other girls rebelling against any restraint and following the lead of Masha who, already thirteen, openly smoked cigarettes and blatantly passed on to some of the far younger girls she led a bottle of cheap vodka she drank from, as well as ecstasy pills.

In Kira's earliest years, Emilija had sometimes left Kira when still a baby alone behind the firmly locked door of their two rooms when she went about her work cleaning. That had come to an end with a visit from a child welfare officer answering the complaint of someone unknown in Emilija's building who'd been alarmed by the baby crying too long.

With no day-care center near, Emilija, in preschool years, had then been forced to take Kira to work with her, endlessly trying to keep Kira unobtrusively close by her side when a mere toddler, or later stowed away in one way or another so as to be rarely seen, first with a picture book, later with a child's tablet she'd saved for months to buy.

And all the time finding ways to explain to Kira herself why she didn't have the expensive toys or clothes the wealthier children had in homes they visited, or why she and her mother couldn't live the same way. And painfully too Emilija suffered the child's embarrassment at her broken English whenever Emilija dropped her off at school or when taking her along to the convenience store for food.

Especially hard was her cleaning work at the wealthy Carleson home, where she was constantly aware of her real child, Kira, become Cassandra and enjoying everything that she now also wanted for Cassandra become Kira, with all the mother's love she had grown to have for the other woman's child. More than once she had thought to quit the Carlesons, but they paid more than anyone and she was always able, with the help of the cook, who hated Mrs. Carleson, to steal away with enough groceries to cover several days' meals for herself and her stolen daughter.

The benefits of free meals, which slightly alleviated the stress of taking Kira to work with her, finally came to an end with the start of school. But only for a while. As school proceeded from kindergarten to first grade, there'd been the all too frequent complaints from teachers about Kira's sometimes disruptive behavior in class, and once a complaint that Kira was a neglected child when Kira began running loose when school was over, not waiting for Emilija to pick her up and then frequently seen about the area alone and suspected of filching junk food from store shelves.

But worse than anything, far worse than her mother's appearance and broken English, was Kira's awareness of her and her mother's lowly status in life. Kira found it sheer torture when teachers or anyone else asked what her mother did for work. Cornered when with others she was asked to write a short essay about how each saw their mothers, she wrote one time that Emilija was a hospital nurse, and on another that she was a bus driver, and that she yearned for anything above her lowly status.

Lying alone in the dark this night with only the usual sounds from other apartments around her, Emilija felt all the heart-wrenching sadness of being so often rejected by the child she had grown to love so much. It was as though she were being punished for the child not being her own but stolen from another woman and another home. Sleep seemed impossible and more and more she vainly wondered what trouble Kira might be up to, the danger Masha might have led Kira and the gang into.

It was right in the middle of her imagining that Kira had finally come home and had snuggled into bed next to her and said lovingly, as always, "Good night, Mom," when Emilija suddenly began to feel ill. A kind of tense nausea began to spread outward through her body from what began as a first mild discomfort then pain in her chest.

Struggling against a sudden difficulty in breathing, her thoughts turned from anxiety about Kira's onrushing teens and the coming years when her child would become involved first with unwitting boys out for scoring whenever possible, and then with men, Emilija began to remember her own teen years in Lithuania, the warm tenderness of her mother, the laughter of her hardworking father, some of the likes and dislikes she'd experienced in the village of Akniste in the Salakas region with other girls her age. Voices that seemed another life echoed, her memories jumbled, until she suddenly felt nothing but pain.

Eight

When Kira came home, it was late, and it was only after she had drunk vodka with girlfriends and some boys Masha had allowed into their abandoned warehouse hideaway in the Baltic Ghetto They were passing around a bottle, and trying ecstasy, and vaping too, until she had almost allowed one boy to get himself off in her. With no small effort, she desperately thought as she went home how to conceal from her mother, if she were still awake, her dizzy desire to reel about joyfully, and was relieved when, by the faint light of a streetlight below their rooms, she saw her mother asleep.

"I'm home, Mom," she heard herself half-whisper as she pulled back the covers on her side of the bed, and not bothering to undress because it was so cold, she crawled under them and pressed close to her mother for more warmth.

Except there wasn't any warmth from her mother. Her mother felt cold too.

"Mom?" Surprise, then alarm swept through Kira. "Mom?" she repeated. And then sat up, throwing the covers back and putting a hand to her mother's forehead and then to her cold rigid shoulders.

She had hardly realized that Emilija wasn't responding and wouldn't when the first scream rose up from her. First just a scream, then a cry of "Mom. Mom. Mom, wake up. Mom!"

The first person to be aroused by Kira's cries was the old man named Ernest Brezenski, who called home the one small room directly across the hall. He had come from Russia only ten years ago and had found work in the city looking for and exterminating rats.

At first only half asleep, but finally awakened by the screams barely muffled by his and the old Lithuanian woman's doors, he rose as the screams continued. Annoyed to anger to have had his sleep disturbed, he left his room to pound on the door of the two rooms the screams were coming from.

"For Christ's sake, shut the fuck up." And then, "Hey, you in there," his Russian-accented English thick with anger. "Stop with the fucking screams, okay?"

Getting no answer to either his shouts or his pounding on the door, he came fully awake and began to realize something was wrong.

"Fucking old woman and her brat," he muttered angrily in Russian, and returning to his bed, he buttoned 911 on his cell phone. The cops would shut them up.

The response by the alerted police was slow. They were all too often called out into the night by reports of family fights, of husbands beating wives, of drunken brawls and the screaming of mistreated children, to act with any undue haste.

Two cops from the local precinct, one badly overweight, eventually made it up the four flights of stairs to find not just Brezenski but three other tenants, all in their nightclothes and awakened by Brezenski's shouting and pounding for quiet from the now silent room where only the sound of muffled sobs was heard.

"Police. Open up," wasn't answered, so one of the cops kicked open the easily forced door, where, by the hall light, he saw the ten-year-old figure of Kira huddled sobbing on the floor next to the bed and the still uncovered form of Elijia.

"Oh, shit," one cop managed, thoroughly annoyed at what he knew would be the paperwork ahead. He put in a call for an ambulance while his partner, after making certain of death, ordered everyone back to bed. Neither paid any attention to the crying child. Kids her age were in general as much of a pain in the ass to cops in the area as teenagers.

Attention to Kira was left to one of the three uniformed medics who came up the stairs with a stretcher. A burly woman, she first bent over Kira, then seeing her age, knelt beside her. "You okay, honey? Yes?" And then getting no response, and seeing trouble if the child tried to kill herself or proved seriously ill—you never could predict either—said, "Up you get, kid. I think you'd better come with us."

Kira could only think first of Emilija, whose rigid coldness terrified her. Her fear for her mother, the cold deadness and lack of any response in the old woman, grew into a frightening awareness for the first time of being alone, fear for herself, fear of facing all the people, schoolteachers, police, storekeepers, neighbors, all those whom her mother had always protected her from: all those and the people where her mother cleaned, where the servants always seemed menacing, even when offering a tolerant smile.

Dazed with fear, she found herself first in an ambulance, hiding under a bench, then seated on the floor in the brightly lit corridor of a hospital morgue, the gurney with her mother on it only a few feet away. Her head pounded, from ecstasy and vodka, and she shivered with cold until a passing attendant realized she belonged to the death that had just been brought in.

"Your mom they brought in?" Mom was a guess, he thought. Possibly a grandmother. And when Kira lifted her tearful face to simply stare blankly, he said, "On your feet, kid." and pulled Kira up by an arm as at the same time he drew back the sheet on the gurney, exposing Emilija's head and shoulders while demanding, "Yours?"

For the first time Kira saw her mother clearly, the pale drawn tired face of the woman old before her years who was Mom and had been with her for as long as she could remember. She wanted to call out to her to say, "Mom, wake up. It's me." Her fear of her mother as someone dead disappeared, and she only felt an almost overcoming fear in the silence between them of her mother disappearing forever.

Impulsively, she grabbed one of Emilija's cold hands and pulled it close to her. "Mom," she whispered, "Don't go away. Please don't go."

A voice came between her and Emilija. "You know her name?"

"I told the cops."

"Okay. That's enough, then." the morgue attendant pulled Kira away and the sheet back over Emilija's dead face and white hair. And Kira was alone again, the gurney pushed away through double doors, her mother only a form covered by a white sheet. She sank back down on the floor into a numbed silence until she heard a man say, "How did that kid get in here?"

"Dunno. Sneaked into the ambulance with the body."

"Can't be more than ten or eleven. Anybody get in touch with welfare?"

"Medics already have. Lady's down talking to the cops."

Welfare? That was some rotten hole somewhere two of the girls in her gang had escaped from and told everyone about. It was where they put you, sometimes until you were eighteen. Some building with a lot of other girls all with cots in the same room and strict rules about everything until they found a foster home to put you in. One of the girls said the man in the foster home she'd been sent to had held her down, she said, "and tried to put his big thing in my mouth, and not just once."

Streetwise, it took Kira moments to silently evade the cops talking to the welfare lady by the ambulance that was just pulling away into the darkness of the streets beyond the hospital.

She found the door open to the two rooms she shared with her mother, the lock wrecked by the police when they entered, and the building silent with its tenants returned to bed in their own rooms. If the police should come back, it wouldn't be before daylight, she decided, and she silently, and without turning on a light, found and put a few things in her backpack, took away her mother's old thread-bare coat, and then began a search for the money saved from earnings she knew her mother had kept carefully stowed away, dollar by dollar.

She found it, finally, carefully hidden in a coffee can that had been pushed way back out of sight behind clothes on the top shelf of the cupboard in which her mother had hung her old salvaged winter coat and her two dresses.

Kira counted the money, six hundred and

forty-five dollars. In the kitchen, she found a plastic bag, carefully folded and put the money into it, and then hid the bag away as deep in the pocket of her mother's old coat as she could.

She had time, she thought, until the welfare people and the cops caught up with her. She'd hide out in the gang's warehouse and could sleep there for a while to stay out of the winter cold, and there was always the easily lifted food from the convenience store.

Satisfied she'd got everything, Kira stole away from the dismal two rooms of her childhood and stood for a moment in the icy hallway, uncertain. Wearing her mother's old coat but shivering now with cold, she thought of the years of trying to cook on the ancient two-burner gas stove, of schoolwork at the wooden kitchen table, of the sagging bed she shared with her mother.

A sound from somewhere in the old building jarred her back to reality and the empty streets below, the warehouse blocks away. After a moment and not looking back, she closed the door on the two rooms that had been her life with Emilija Paulauskas, who had loved and cared for her, and went down the stairs. She was on her own.

Nine

Detective Alter Weiss, seated at his desk in the police precinct office, found it hard to listen seriously to Grace Garrity's argument for bringing in a suspect in a store robbery for an interview. He knew it would get them nowhere; the suspect was a hardened criminal who would use all the tricks of avoidance when interviewed, and Weiss's mind was on his success in discovering the full name of the woman revealed by Father Andrew in the priest's report of her confession.

But Grace, however, being tied up in an interview, gave him time to look further for information on the woman he now knew was named Paulauskas, and when Grace was gone, Weiss made some necessary phone calls and took off himself.

At city records, and with the little knowledge of any date other than it being somewhere between twenty and thirty-five years ago, he eventually came across a birth record for Cassandra Carleson, a daughter born to Rowena and Arthur Carleson. The date and name confirmed that both girls were now in their mid-twenties. There was no record, however, of a child born to a mother named Emilija Paulauskas, which clearly indicated that her child had first seen the light of day most likely at home without a doctor and perhaps not even a midwife.

Lack of official record of the child's existence forcibly brought home the reality that there was some young woman somewhere who, if not dead, was in her twenties and bore a name that didn't belong to her. Was that name still Paulauskas, and if not, what was it? And far more importantly, what had become of her since she was forcibly placed with a mother not her own?

"Where the hell do I go from here?" Weiss asked his wife when he told her what he'd found.

"That's a rhetorical question, Alt. You'll know better than anyone after you check death records for the Paulauskas woman, and that's if, in this precinct, you find any."

Which Weiss soon did. In the city's death records he found several registered deaths with the name of Paulauskas but only one with a first name of Emilija. She had died sixteen years ago, with her death listed as cardiac seizure. But more interesting to the detective than the death date of the

Lithuanian cleaning woman was her address.

Could the child she'd stolen conceivably still be living there? And if she wasn't and had long since gone, could there be any tenant who had been there while Emilija Paulauskas was living and who would remember if she'd had a child?

The next time Detective Weiss had a few free hours and was relieved momentarily from his over-eager partner's endless persistence, he went to the building listed in the city records as the address of the death of Emilija Paulauskas.

Alter Weiss was used to the poverty in his Baltic Ghetto precinct, and saw the street of the building he searched for as perfectly normal for the area. No street lamps, uncollected garbage piled up in alley-ways or in unemptied dumpsters, no numbers on doorways, and a notable absence of fire escapes out-side most of the five-story brownstone buildings.

Just the same, he was a little taken aback by the equally run-down condition of the inside of the building, where he hoped to find information on a young woman who to him might still be Pau-lauskas. The stairwell lights didn't work, and the place, besides dampness and linoleum worn away from floors, had the cold silence of a tomb, until he heard a door slam on the floor above him.

He headed for it, and guessing what door it was, knocked on it hard, and was rewarded by a surprisingly respectable looking elderly woman in a dress and apron whom he had obviously inter-rupted while cooking.

Weiss knew the form, apologized profusely, showed his police ID, and asked if the woman could supply him with any information whatsoever about a former tenant who had died around twenty years ago. No, she was sorry, she said. She couldn't, but maybe Mr. Brezenski could. He lived one flight up, in a room right above hers. "And good luck," she said, "if he's there. He's very old and has an ugly temper."

Thanking the woman, Weiss went up one flight, and to a door directly above hers, and knocked. Not once but several times and then even more. He had given up and had turned away when the door opened abruptly and a quavering voice angrily demand to know who he was and what he wanted.

Weiss spun around to see a very elderly man, clothed only in underpants, standing just inside the door, with a look of fury in his eyes. Certain he was wasting his time. Weiss again showed his ID and said he was seeking information about a woman named Emilija Paulauskas who had once lived in the building. The result of his questioning was a surprise. The man instantly looked more than furious. "That bitch and her fucking brat? Left here years ago, thank God."

A few more curses, answers to only a few more questions, but when Weiss left the building, it was with the satisfaction that he had not only learned that Emilija had lived just down the hall but had died there too. "Place was filled with medics and fucking cops," the old man ranted, "and that was the end of them both."

But checking police records, Weiss came up empty-handed. The cops who came the night the old lady died had taken advantage of the woman's near anonymity to never enter her death in their log books, nor did he find any mention of her daughter in the police database. Both had long since retired or transferred to a different precinct, and Weiss knew it would be futile to look them up.

"Well, that's hardly nothing," Weiss's wife, Dana, said that evening when Alter Weiss told her how far he'd come along in his search. "And so you've got to our Cassandra become Kira and only just eleven. What's next?"

"The lucky one who today is named Cassandra Carleson," her husband said.

"And not the Cassandra become Kira? Easy way out." His wife laughed. "Shame on you."

"Yeah, I know," Weiss replied, "but trying to find a street kid with only the name Paulauskas to go by is a bottomless pit, if indeed she still goes by such a name. She could have changed it to avoid welfare officers or later married someone.

"Going the current Cassandra living with Arthur Carleson and wife route," he continued, "might be a momentary distraction, but it could at least sew up any mystery about that child until I get some more information of what happened to the Kira one, whom I've lost any traces of after her mother died. Where she went, somebody must know, so I'll just have to keep at it, and in the meanwhile check with Grace and see what she's come up with."

"Grace?"

"Yeah, I've got her looking into the Carleson child, but strictly off the record."

Alter Weiss had no possible way of knowing Grace had already come up with far more about Cassandra than expected.

Ten

"Happy Birthday to you. Happy birthday, dear Cassie. Happy birthday to you."

Taking a deep breath, Cassandra blew out the eleven candles on the cake amidst the laughing cheers of six of her friends from Knightsbridge Hall, the exclusive boarding school to which she had been sent that year.

It was supposed to be a joyous occasion, and certainly had all the appearances of one, and was celebrated at Quarters, the family country home, an enormous six-bedroom house in rolling horse country an hour from the city. The party with her school friends had been managed with considerable difficulty in arranging school permission and transport for each girl by Miss Miller, her mother's private secretary, who supervised not only her mother's trips abroad and purchases but was in charge of all social arrangements while ruling all the servants with an iron hand as well.

The party was a big success, but the moment all the girls were gone, any appearances of good will where Cassandra was concerned came to an end. The morning after the party, Cassandra rose at dawn to face the day after a near sleepless night of emotion that was half anger and resentment. Risking punishment for riding without permission, she sneaked out of the house before anyone else was up and went to the stables to saddle up her own horse, Stormy, with whom she then enjoyed a fast canter in the freshening early morning air, only stopping for a moment atop one hill to watch the sun rise above the far horizon.

There, for a few minutes, she was able to forget the nasty scene she'd had with her father before all the girls had come for the birthday party and she'd had to go with him and her mother to a required meeting at boarding school with the Knightsbridge Hall headmistress, Miss Goodwin, who managed the lives and education of some three hundred girls for nine months of every year.

Her father had canceled his own appointment for a business meeting, and her mother had made a rare appearance for the first time, as Miss Goodwin had asked both parents to be present, if possible, and Cassandra too.

The headmistress, wearing her perpetual

condescending smile to hide any and every disciplinary revelation, had clearly enjoyed saying, "I'm sure, Mr. and Mrs. Carleson, that Cassandra understands that an attack on anyone by any of the girls isn't behavior we can ever condone at Knightsbridge Hall."

Cassandra had sat in silence, choking back all the unfairness of the meeting. She had head-butted the soccer coach below the waist because he had wrongly, as usual, benched her best friend, Arielle, for not paying attention at one of his "talks," and had threatened her with the same for rising to Arielle's defense.

Throughout the meeting, she had listened, numbed, to Miss Goodwin's accusations of other breeches in discipline, etiquette, her arguing with teachers, and her absence from required attendance at chapel. And she had suffered a threat launched by Miss Goodwin. The headmistress had seemed unafraid of Cassandra's parents.

"Cassandra," she said, "would learn to keep her anger at discipline to herself. Or else."

Worse than any of the meeting was her father's icy affirmation, birthday or no, of everything said by Miss Goodwin the moment they returned home.

"Your behavior is unacceptable, Cassandra, and I don't want to hear any reports of your stepping out of line like that again, either at school or here at home from Miss Baldweig."

Miss Baldweig was the new governess who had appeared a month earlier to replace old Cissy, her many years' English nanny. Knowing that her father could see nothing wrong in anything the German governess might do, which he had emphasized on her appearance by saying, "Some good German discipline will soon calm you down, young lady," Cassandra had, as always, sat in seething silence. She had learned from her first day of the governess's tenure that any whistle-blowing about her strict German discipline would bring swift punishment from her father, then retaliation from the governess herself.

"It's not fair," she said to Stormy, stroking the horse's neck and dallying where they had halted to allow Cassandra to further collect herself before heading back to the stable and then the house, where, pretending she had just emerged from her bedroom, she ate a silent breakfast at the dining room table, which was large enough to comfortably seat eight but where she sat alone but supervised by Miss Baldweig.

Finished with breakfast, Cassandra spent the day back at the stable with Tommy, the ageing black Labrador, who rarely left her side, and with only a brief glimpse of her mother while conjuring up every excuse possible to keep Miss Baldweig, unfamiliar with horses, at a distance, whether the stable activity she came up with was necessary or not.

The German governess was a big woman with a plain face that rarely smiled. She wore her hair snubbed back in a knot and too much lipstick, and her breath always smelled. At school, when

Cassandra described her, Ariella said, "You have a governess, Cassie? Jeepers, what for?"

"To teach me how to disobey," Cassandra had replied, laughing. But even as she laughed, Cassandra didn't feel there was anything to laugh about where the governess was concerned. Any defiance of Miss Baldweig meant defiance of her father. And defying Arthur Carleson simply wasn't what anybody did. One recent column in the state's leading newspaper was devoted to his firing fifty employees for daring to strike and picket, something that brought acid comments from Arielle at school. Arielle was an avid reader of the news, on top of everything she saw on television. And she constantly took up verbal arms for the underdog.

Even at the age of eleven, Cassandra Carleson, for all her wealthy upbringing, was beginning to learn how to stand up to whatever she felt was injustice, and in doing so predict how much defending the underdog would mean in her future.

Eleven

Cassandra's following years at Knightsbridge Hall were marked by occasional and sporadic incidents of her fighting back against whatever she saw as unfairness. She was faced more than once with being called into the headmistress's office, the headmistress having become a Miss Pruitt, who had replaced Miss Godwin, who had departed from Knightsbridge Hall to assume a deanship at a college in another state.

"No argument, Cassandra. Your behavior was unacceptable."

"But, Miss Pruit."

"Enough. I don't want to see you in here again."

Cassandra reluctantly left Miss Pruitt's s office, feeling as always that her side of things would never be heard, even when criticism of her behavior with boys seemed totally unjust. Boys to Cassandra were something new and, in her case, their presence occurred twice a year when they came from Onslow, an elitist boys boarding school, to participate in supervised formal dances with the girls at Knightsbridge Hall. Almost immediately Cassandra found herself in trouble for the way she danced with one boy in particular on whom she had an instant crush.

What was wrong with her dancing snuggled close to the boy when they were dancing, his body hard against hers, and her filled with a newly experienced tingle of excitement? Grownups in the movies and on television went many steps farther than dancing close to a boy.

Almost worse than the sharp rebuke she'd received for it was the emptiness she experienced when the boy had gone back to Onslow, her feeling of an unrequited yearning that saw nights filled with never before experienced emotions that took weeks to subside and was often made worse in the after-lights-out giggling and whispering of other girls about what they could do with boys later when finally free of boarding school, and imagining sex with someone, especially with the pop star, Sandy Summer, whose latest album had gone off the charts.

There was relief in sports, and she excelled at lacrosse, her aggressive playing bringing the Knightsbridge Hall team one victory after another in games they played against other girls schools, but more than once saw her sidelined by referees for fouls, while her victories were never mentioned or praised at home.

The end of her third year at Knightsbridge Hall also spelled the end of Miss Baldweig, with the hated German governess simply not there one day, and to Cassandra's everlasting joy with nobody replacing her, except and on very rare occasions, Miss Miller. It also spelled the strengthening of her friendship with Arielle, a devoted girlfriend and objector to rules of any kind, but a girl clever enough to stay out of trouble.

And there was the deep relief and happiness to be experienced in yet another summer among the many spent for as long as she could remember by the sea with Grandma Mary in the old house and life she shared with Grandfather Henry.

Grandma Mary was a serious reader, and the house was lined with books. There was sailing with Grandpa Henry in the Cape Cod sloop moored by the float at the end of the pier that extended from the lawn separating their house from the water, while on the lawn there were often exciting croquet games with both grandparents. Best of all there was a month with never a word of reprimand or word of rebuke.

But that joy was dispelled in her senior year at boarding school by the death of Tommy, her companion since earliest childhood, and almost immediately afterward, the sudden disappearance of her beloved Stormy. Cassandra came home from her grandparents, unwarned and unprepared, to find her father had summarily closed down the stables, selling off all five horses and dismissing her long loyal friend, Charlie, the stable master who had been an endless source of excitement, with stories of his early prior life as a jockey.

Less painful to Cassandra but more of a surprise and a shock, her senior year also saw the end of her parent's marriage, which she learned of right before Christmas and only months after they were divorced, when it was confirmed by Miss Miller after she received the surprise of a brief letter from her mother, which was really nothing more than a cryptic note announcing that she had obtained a divorce in the Virgin Islands. It meant nothing to Cassandra, to whom her mother had never been more than a name and a slightly mysterious authority whom she rarely saw.

But knowledge of the divorce brought something else entirely unwelcome: news first of an unexpected interest in her father's life, then a fact that was almost immediately proved to be even worse.

This was the abrupt arrival of a stepmother, Helen, who, when Cassandra came home on spring vacation, was simply there with no warning, a virtual stranger occupying Cassandra's mother's room and all the rest of the house as well, and who wasted no time in telling Cassandra that she expected the same disciplined behavior from her as her father did.

Cassandra detested the woman from the moment she laid eyes on her as she prepared herself for college, and she steered clear of her as much as possible, seeing Helen only at meals, although with the stable and horses gone, that proved difficult, and which she managed only by keeping up a close school friendship with Arielle.

Arielle had a driving license, and during vacation times the use of one of her family's cars. She lived not far away, and with her freedom from parents who seemed not to be concerned with her many absences, which they regarded as normal in a seventeen-year-old, she quite openly carried on an all-the-way romance with an Onslow boy who lived in the same area.

And Cassandra, taking advantage of being largely ignored at home due to her father's new marriage, enjoyed drinking and ecstasy and her first sexual experience, which lasted some weeks with another former boarding school boy who summered not far away and who seemed daringly free to do whatever he wished. As an added attraction, he drove an expensive convertible sports car.

She and Arielle formed a four person group with the two boys, enjoying as a foursome movies and pizzas at a local joint, adventuresome nights dancing at a famed mostly teens nightclub, with late night swimming in one boy's pool when his parents were absent, and sometimes stripping completely before diving into the water.

For Cassandra, it marked her throwing off childhood, and in spite of finally finishing school at Knightsbridge Hall, convincing herself that she was now a grown-up woman far more experienced in life than anyone else there, including the teachers, whom she saw as old-maid nothings.

Twelve

ollege finally came, with Knights-bridge Hall and its hated headmistress and teachers as well finally a thing of the troubled past. As expected, Cassandra's grades were nowhere near high enough for acceptance at Hanover, the prestigious university attended in his youth by her father. Cassandra was accepted, however, simply because her father was a powerful member of the university's board of trustees, a towering alumnus in his generosity as a financial donor and a political lobbyist. A principal building devoted to its flourishing business school bore his name along with the that of the school itself.

Cassandra found his importance embarrassing, however. During her last two years at Knights-bridge Hall, she had become politically aware of the power of wealth that big business had over so much of the lives of so many people, the way her father had aways had over her, and she only allowed herself to be registered by her inseparable friend Arielle, whose high grades opened the door of the prestigious university for her and who was blunt in her persuasive urging.

"Fuck 'em, Cassie. Who gives a flying shit how important all the goddamned alumni are, especially your old man. The university's name once you are out of the place will virtually guarantee you a job, and you can become an activist like me and use the university name to help fight for women's rights against all the unrestrained heavy male hands of those in power."

And there was freedom from the endless supervision and rules, which Cassandra had come to see as tyranny in all its restrictions and personal invasion when still back in school. With Stormy gone, she had never been able to escape in her early morning rides when at times she felt nearly suffocated. Now there were no bedtimes or mealtimes, with the only times you had to respect the times of your various classes and lectures. Unrestrained, Cassandra found herself actually enjoying some of what she was being taught.

And there was the wonderful freedom of nearly all-night gatherings not just with girls but with outspoken boys who stoked campus activist fires with their unafraid aggressive enthusiasm.

One of them was Archie Kramer, a blunt-spoken, working-class fireball whose father worked in a steel mill notorious for its dangerous working conditions and endless labor unrest. Spotted at once amidst any student body gathering at Hanover due to his forever shaggy unkempt hair that fell uncombed to below his chin and around his lean hungry face, Archie had achieved admission to the university through affirmative action as well as his exceptionally high grades in high school. He had only been attending classes for a month when he had organized a group known as SFF, Students for Freedom.

And Cassandra, who met him at one of its meetings, found in him a companion in her now long-held resistance to authority of nearly any kind but a physical love also. She was not only soon spending more nights in his dormitory room than in her own, and with virtually no interest in any further education, she nevertheless followed him into postgraduate studies in politics.

It was Archie's relentless influence that caused the always existing embers of revolt in Cassandra to finally burst into flame and cause a dramatic end to her educational years as well as to her background of wealth and privilege.

It was a Students for Freedom assembly and march at the state capital on the Fourth of July that provided the fuel for the explosion. Getting close to the dome-roofed capitol building, shouting their slogans and protests, the SFF group of nearly two hundred workers and veteran activists had first merged with a large group protesting for women's and LGBTQ rights and abortion laws to demand much more: the end to government they saw run by the vested interests of big money.

Violently emotional, their march came to an abrupt halt when finally confronted by a line of state police troopers who had little sympathy for them and their grievances. The protesters were not to be stopped, and Cassandra among them lost all control of herself in using the staff of the flag she was carrying as a spear and a club to get her close enough in the melee to a police car to throw a Molotov cocktail through one of its open windows. As it burst into flame, a trooper's taser brought her to her knees. She was seized, roughly manacled helpless, and thrown into a police van along with others.

Obliged to yield to the forces of law, Cassandra felt them to its fullest extent when she was booked for dangerous assault on a state trooper, along with arson in the destruction of the police car, and she heard the heavy iron clang of a cell door shutting on her.

Thirteen

Susan Watkins was a registered nurse who had become the public official in charge of the city's child welfare division. Known mostly as Nurse Watkins and at middle age long experienced with all the harshness of life, she was a warm and kindly woman especially concerned with the well-being of the many children she had rescued from homelessness, abuse by adults, or drug and alcohol addiction.

A bleak wintery day found her on her way to the building squeezed amid the warehouses of the city's outskirts that housed the children's welfare division, where rescued children were momentarily kept until placed in foster homes. She'd stopped her car to avoid being an obstacle to a very large truck bearing down on her on the narrow street she was on and was waiting for the truck to pass, when glancing at the sidewalk, she happened to catch movement in an unused section of culvert by an abandoned building project.

Leaving her car when the truck had gone, Nurse Watkins realized that what she had seen was a flutter of movement inside the culvert, and ever curious and deciding at once that it wasn't some sort of large animal, she left her car to approach the culvert to take a closer look. She quickly realized that it was part of a large cardboard box she'd seen and that half covered the huddled figure of a young girl partially wrapped in a shabby cloth coat.

Nurse Watkins was shocked. She was used to homelessness, to people sleeping in doorways or right on the sidewalk wrapped in blankets and newspapers. But this? A child out in this sort of weather with snow on the ground and with only an old cloth coat and a strip of cardboard for warmth?

She knelt by the child who she saw at once was a girl ten or eleven years old and one who looked not just pathetically ragged, her hair in unwashed tangles, smudges of dirt and soot on her face and hands, but was dangerously cold.

Sue leaned close. "Hello, there. Can you wake up? Aren't you terribly cold?"

There was no answer. The nurse tried again.

"You need to get warm. And don't be afraid of me. I'm a registered nurse."

Kira finally stirred and looked up at the smiling close-to-her woman.

"That's better," the nurse said. "Let's get you to my car and some warmth. I may have something to eat left over from lunch in it."

There was no answer, just a wide-eyed and frightened look. Until Nurse Watkins said, "What's your name? Mine's Sue."

She waited and got a one-word answer.

"Kira."

The name took the nurse by surprise but she recognized it as being an old Lithuanian one long out of favor. The girl must have come from the crowded slum of different Baltic peoples back in the city.

"Well, come on, Kira. I'm not going to let you lie here and freeze. Up you get." She pulled Kira to her feet and took her firmly by the hand to her car.

Inside, she quickly pulled the child's threadbare old cloth coat tight round her legs and covered her body with her own down jacket.

"There we are. Isn't that better?

"She got out the thermos of still warm coffee she'd left unfinished and poured some into its unscrewed top, which she pressed it into the child's icy hands.

"You were dangerously close to hyperthermia, young lady," she said.

Kira didn't know what that meant, but she knew kindness when she heard it. And help when she'd given up and crawled into the culvert as a refuge after an angry Masha had ejected her from the gang's hideout for refusing to join in the theft of a convenience store. In the warmth of the car, as the nurse continued on her way to the welfare home, Kira barely heard her ask again who she was.

She didn't answer. Her thoughts jumbled back to the cold, still figure of her mother, to the cops who'd come, and then seeing her mother first in the ambulance, then under the sheet on the gurney.

She remembered a voice, asking who she was and saying to someone "Better get this one off to Welfare," and then herself in a police car until she was in an office someplace being questioned.

"Your name? Mother's name, father's name? Address? Your birthday? Which school do you go to?"

She remembered suddenly feeling all the questions were a danger to her mother, the woman and man asking them and writing down her answers in scrawled notes on some official form, making it look as if her mother had done something wrong in dying. She kept seeing her mother's cold still form huddled beneath the blanket.

When she was granted bathroom permission and her questioners' backs were turned, she fled.

And now, when Nurse Watkins pulled up and said, "Here we are," Kira saw the same building from which she had just stolen away from and panicked. The frightened cry came involuntarily out of her with the words, "No, no. Please."

The nurse stopped her just in time from scrambling out of the car. She held Kira firmly and demanded to know what was wrong.

Kira's crying plea had turned into helpless sobs. "I have to go to the church."

"The church?"

"Back in town. Father Andrew. Please, please."

Nurse Watkins had hardly remembered that there was an elderly Father Andrew at the Church of St. Mary Magdelene when Kira pulled the plastic bag with her mother's money from a pocket of the old coat protecting her legs. She heard the girl say between sobs that the money was to bury her mother in the churchyard, "so she won't end up in in some unmarked grave in potter's field."

Susan Watkins had experienced nearly everything imaginable in her job officiating over the welfare of lost, abandoned, or simply runaway children. But a homeless eleven-year-old wanting to bring money to a church with which to bury her mother?

A minute later, and brought up short by the desperation she heard in the girl's voice, she turned her car around and headed back into the city for the old Church of St. Mary Magdelene.

Fourteen

Without her realizing it—she had been too busy keeping a roof over hers and her child's head to think about anything else—Emilija Paulauskas had forced on Kira an awareness that life for the lowly-born, more often than not, consisted mostly of years of hard labor and that nothing else was possible.

All this was already glaringly obvious to Kira when she was placed in her first foster home by the children's welfare office. Wise beyond her years not just from roaming the city's backstreets with the gang she'd been in that was always looking for trouble and often finding it, there had also been the constant example set for her by her Lithuanian immigrant mother's endless struggle to bring home food, to pay rent, and to clothe herself and her child, all without education or fluency in the strange language every immigrant found themselves surrounded by.

Forever embarrassed by her mother's thick accent and the work she did, cleaning offices and other people's toilets, Kira nevertheless was always filled with returning the love and caring that her mother forever showed her.

The foster parents she was placed with were Donald and Barbara Doyle. The couple were an ordinary middle-class working pair whose home was four rooms in a modern, recently built working-class apartment building. Donald, an overweight and loose-fleshed licensed electrician, was welcoming friendliness itself, while his wife, Barbara, who worked behind the counter at a fast-food Burger King, was the opposite, a narrow, rather tight-faced woman.

With Barbara unable to have a child, the couple were seeking to adopt when their financial and social stability was looked into, then verified by the welfare council as stable by council's homeless child office, and Kira was placed with them.

It took Kira some time to adjust to the step up in living from the two cold and barren rooms she had shared for as long as she could remember in the run-down building in the Baltic Ghetto. It took time to become used to being so close to two people she first saw as strangers to be avoided, and who were so different from her mother. It took time to feel safe to the strangeness of a bed of her own, to have a cooked meal at night before the newness of watching television, to adjust to having something else completely new in her life, a bath in a bathtub.

But she slowly adjusted to easier living than she had ever known, to safety and a sense of belonging somewhere. She began to lose her feeling of being totally alone, and even though she couldn't bring herself to like the man and his wife, while pretending that she did, to accept that life with the Doyles was what life was supposed to be.

That newfound safety came to an end, however, one night when Kira was in the bathtub after dinner, her mind completely on what had gone on that day in school and on the warmth of the bathwater. She had just soaped a washcloth when she became aware of someone in the doorway and that it was not Barbara but Donald who was standing silently staring at her with an odd smile on his face.

He was gone after moment but reappeared at several subsequent bath times until one day Kira saw the fly of his trousers wide open and Doyle beginning to fondle himself, while right behind him, her arm around his waist, was Barbara, who wore a strange smile.

Everything in Kira froze. She'd seen enough men urinating between parked cars or right out in the open when with her gang, which often shouted laughing insults at them, to be familiar with men's sex. But a man she was supposed to call father and his wife too? A scream of fear rose up out and then her frantic shouts of "Go away" and

"Shut the door," while she sank protectively deep in the bathwater.

When Doyle and his wife retreated, a frightened Kira emerged from the bath and protected herself with a towel while the couple she was supposed to see as father and mother made an immediate pretense of having done nothing wrong and a show of wondering why Kira was upset.

But Kira wasn't fooled. The creepy incident with them killed any further feeling of safety in their four rooms. She could no longer even think of being near either Doyle or his wife. She could only think of getting away, and one night, the moment their bedroom door shut on them, she silently stuffed her few clothes into her backpack and fled, even while certain she'd now be in trouble with the welfare council when they found out.

There was brief respite when she'd crawled humbly back to her former gang and begged to be allowed to sleep in their hideaway. That meant the basement room in the mostly empty storage warehouse, where upstairs there was still running water and a toilet. It was a meeting place where the girls hid stolen food and anything else they could get money for at the pawn shop whose shady owner knew that asking questions would see his shop window smashed the next day.

With no place else to go, Kira slept nights in the mostly empty building, cowering in the cold when she'd hear a truck and then the voices of men who had come late to take away heavy storage. But there was one good meal each day and safety at school, however, when she managed to sneak back into it, her few days absence unnoticed.

But her freedom didn't last long. She was spotted one night by two cops in a patrol car who found a child her age alone on the streets suspicious. When she started to run from them, they seized her and returned her to the welfare council home where all her lingering fear that one of the Doyles was certain to appear at any moment to demand her return was dispelled by a furious Nurse Watkins, who made no secret of her determination to see police action against both Doyle and his wife.

Within days, Kira was placed in another foster home, this time with a couple who had tragically lost a previous homeless child they'd taken in to a pedestrian accident. Their grieving for the loss behind them, they were actively looking for another child to replace her.

They were a Herman and Annette Danziger, Herman the burly warm-hearted owner of a small transport company, his wife a motherly leader in a number of community projects. And after a first few awkward weeks of settling in to their tidy two-bedroom home on a quiet leafy street of similar houses, Kira's sense of defenselessness and isolation, her fears of all adults, began again to be slowly replaced with glimmers of hope and actual feeling of safety, with her new parents soon fitting her into a routine of having breakfast with Herman Danziger before he went to work, and then of being escorted to school by his smiling wife, who warmly embraced her before seeing her through the school door for the day and who would appear after the closing bell to walk her back to what had become her new home, where there was TV to watch before bedtime and being tucked into a clean and comfortable bed in her own little room with a softly carpeted floor, flowered curtains, and pictures on the walls.

It took days for Kira to once more become used to not being on her own or frightened of adults and the need to hide from her past, and to more and more accept life with the Danzigers, and to forget her too often ashamed life with her mother, the fear she'd suffered with the Doyles, and life in the streets with Masha and the gang.

Something unexpected came out of Kira's turning her back on all that. Aware that she'd moved up from her once lowly status in which everyone had always seemed above her, Kira realized she might just go even farther, and began to dream of a life that could be even better than in the foster home with the Danzigers that good luck had brought her to. She began to dream of the life she often saw led by rich people on television or at the movies that the Danzigers seemed to so admire but never even imagined possible for their kind of people.

Fifteen

ood luck occasionally falls on some more
than once, and such was the case for Kira
when that future above others that she
dreamed came her way again, this time through the
person of Aileen Ford, her fifth-grade teacher.

An unassuming middle-aged woman, Ford had
worked for years in the city's public school system
overseeing the young growth of hundreds of unruly
children. Most, if not every one of them, came from
lower-working-class backgrounds, many from the
Baltic Ghetto, and had little desire to learn anything. For far too many, school was a useful few
hours away from homes that were either abusive
or completely neglectful and where an utter lack of
any decorum or manners was the rule, to say nothing of any thought that life could be better.

Mrs. Ford read the one-page efforts she'd asked her ten- and eleven-year-old students to write. The subject was what they hoped to be in life. With an all-too-usual mixture of boredom and frustration at the shallowness she saw behind every word of almost every paper, *Why do I bother?* was her feeling until she scanned the page written by a student whose name was Kira Paulauskas.

When she returned the papers she's asked to be written, many almost illegible or incoherent, she kept back the one written by Kira, and at the end of the day asked Kira to remain in class a few minutes. What the child had written, and although in a barely legible scrawl, had brought Mrs. Ford up short.

"Class dismissed," she said, and as her pupils grabbed backpacks and coats and scrambled for the door as though escaping from bitter punishment, said, "Not you, Kira. You'll stay a moment, please."

The order stung Kira. What had she done wrong?

Mrs. Ford asked Kira to sit by her desk, smiled at the obviously worried and anxious girl, and holding up Kira's paper, said, "I know you wrote this. Can you talk to me about it?"

Kira managed to stammer out her anxiety.

"Did I say something wrong"?

The teacher refrained from an urge to laugh with sheer pleasure. Seated staring anxiously at her was the child she had hoped for years to find in her fifth-grade class, a ten-year-old who on one page had expressed a yearning for a better life from what she had, a better home, to know and be accepted by better people, to raise herself somehow out of where life had forced her into street gangs and foster homes, to be seen as someone who counted.

Kira Paulauskas was a girl who Mrs. Ford and all the other teachers called a "welfare child," one they knew came from "who knew where," a child who was almost certainly orphaned and was currently lodged by the welfare council in a second foster home. Somehow this child had seen a different and better life for herself, and her determination was to have it. She deserved it if anybody did, Mrs. Ford thought, and the teacher was determined she'd have it. The child just needed the right start.

"Kira, nothing wrong," she said. "Quite the contrary. I wanted to ask you if you'd like to change schools. I think you'd probably like Barnes better than here."

"The question almost stopped Kira from thinking. Barnes, the common name for PS 3 across the city, was a school devoted to promising higher-level students. Few at Kira's current PS 7 ever spoke of it, or if they did, of the impossibility of their ever going there. Barnes was for other kids.

The next day, Kira was summoned to the principal's office to talk to Mr. Cranmore, a severe man whose strict discipline was seen by all eight grades of the middle school as something to avoid at all cost. Ever skeptical of any student's intelligence, and even when confronted by the flat-out demand from Mrs. Ford that he agree to Kira's transfer to Barnes, he stated he'd have to speak to one or both of the girl's foster parents first, and arranged to have either Mr. or Mrs. Danziger summoned.

When several days later both appeared, Herman Danziger looking a little awkward and shy at the strangeness of a school principal's office, which seemed a step above him. Annette Danziger appeared far more confident. The meeting was fairly short when neither expressed any hesitation in affirming what Mrs. Ford had seen in her pupil.

"Barnes, yes, by all means," Annette Danziger stated flatly, her arms folded authoritatively across her ample bosom. "I'm glad someone finally saw Kira's potential."

And then from burly Herman Danziger, surprisingly firm and confident words that said far more than anything that in his own unembarrassed respect for a higher education he'd ever had himself.

"I think," he said, "Barnes should be just a first stop on Kira's way to college."

Sixteen

It was a stop that saw a frightened ten-year-old, who had known little other than severe deprivation, finish not only middle school with honors but high school as well.

At Barnes, Kira found herself in a classroom where no one was causing trouble but instead were hard at work and where teachers helped rather than disciplined. It took a while for her not to feel awkward and out of place among them, and she had almost finished the fifth grade before she got used to no gang fighting nor any of the students smoking, drinking, or secretly sharing drugs.

By the end of middle school, high school, which before Barnes had only been a name and place that, when rarely mentioned, was thought of as somewhere completely foreign and unattainable, found Kira in a new circle of friends who, instead of gathering in darkened streets and planning a theft, partied at someone's house and shared video games and television and gossiped about the latest album by their current pop-star hero.

Kira had landed well when placed determinedly by Nurse Watkins in a good home, where she was enclosed by the parenthood of Herman Danziger and his wife, Annette. From Herman, there was always his low booming voice of encouragement, and going with him to football and soccer games, from a warm and bosomy Annette, the strangeness of shopping in the supermarket and looking for new clothes at Walmart. And both welcoming a girl whom Kira had found friendly and safe enough to know and invite her into their house, which Kira had begun to call home.

Living with the Danzigers, memories of her earliest life with Emilija Paulauskas became a flicker of images like a dying candle in night's darkness but which she never let disappear, however, zealously clinging to her memory of the tired figure of her mother in her old cloth coat taking her along on cleaning jobs and only speaking to her in whispers while keeping her close to her side. Not forgotten were images of her mother finding clothes for her in among the discarded clothes of others in a bin outside The Salvation Army, her mother making the bed they shared, cooking meals on their two-burner gas stove, taking her to St. Mary Magdelene to sit silently in prayer in a pew, and angrily defending herself and Kira against any neighbors in their building who found something to shout at them for.

In an entirely different life with the Danzigers, Kira bit by bit got used to their calling her "their daughter" to their friends, and one day, almost unconsciously, she called Herman Danziger "Dad" and Annette "Mom" while at school. With all traces of her humble Lithuanian origins gone, she was officially known as Kira Danziger.

Herman Danziger's proud confidence about college being a guaranteed future event for Kira became an exciting fact after Kira's high grades and the school principal's recommendation boosted Kira's application via affirmative action into her being rewarded with her acceptance at Ranger, a leading university competitor to Hanover. A high school graduation was celebrated by a gathering of friends and neighbors, with Kira, along with all of them, proud of what she'd accomplished and gratefully aware of who had helped her to do so. At a congratulatory dinner after the graduation ceremony, during which in traditional hat and gown she had celebrated the end of her high school years, she heard Herman Danziger say when he rose to raise his glass at dinner, "Here's to our daughter and all her great future years," emphasizing to Kira herself her belonging not just to her proud Danziger foster parents but to a whole better world of living, far removed from her now barely remembered childhood.

Kira wasted no time in adjusting to the freedom of study she found during her first year of college. She fell easily into campus life that she never quite took for granted, the lack of personal restriction outside of rigorous courses and studying. She lived in classrooms and lecture halls and shared a dormitory room with Rosalind, a girl from a far distant farm state with whom she not only quickly developed a firm and affectionate friendship but something that was entirely new to her: trust.

It was because of Rosalind coming from such a totally different background that Kira for the first time since middle school was forced into sometimes openly dredging up her own past, into revealing what her name had once been, where she had come from, and who her real mother was, along with her lowly status in life.

Influenced by Rosalind's account of her small town life, where Rosalind's father was a doctor and her mother a housewife, the reality of Kira's childhood came back up in one almost stumbling confession after another of her Lithuanian name, of the two rooms she had shared with her mother in the always cold and rat-infested world of the Baltic Ghetto, so terribly different from Rosalind's, and the buzzing activity of the college campus they shared.

"The Danzigers aren't my real parents," she confessed, and told Rosalind about her real mother's coming as an uneducated Lithuanian immigrant into the packed Baltic Ghetto to join

Russian, Estonian, and Latvian beginners as a new American.

"Golly, Kira, I can't imagine your name ever having been Paulauskas." Rosalind seemed in no way bothered by Kira's background. She was too fond of Kira to care where she came from, but she wanted to know, however, "Was your name changed legally to Danziger?"

The unexpected question stumped Kira. It had never occurred to her that her name might have been legally changed. Had it? She couldn't remember, and on her first trip home, she found it difficult although an independent young woman about to graduate college, to ask either of her now almost elderly Danziger parents.

Summoning up her courage, she finally did one night at a quiet dinner with them both, while seated as always around the kitchen table.

There was a moment when neither foster parent answered, until finally Herman Danziger did. No, but they had thought to when they'd become sure of Kira staying with them, although his wife added, they'd been worried for a long time that she might find out and resent them for even considering it.

Her name was still Paulauskas, Herman explained heavily. It was only when Kira was well into high school, he reluctantly admitted, that their fears disappeared, but more importantly with it, their prejudice, which they had come to find ridiculous in their realizing that Kira's name had nothing to do with the child herself, with either her character or personality.

There was a long silence after Herman's and Annette's confession. Tears filled Herman's eyes, Annette bowed her head to stare silently rigid at nothing on the table before her, until Kira, deeply touched by both her parents' obvious emotion over something long hidden, was the first to speak.

Looking at the long-loved faces of both her foster parents, she knew exactly what to say. She would soon leave a loving home and face the world as an independent well-educated young woman. So, she came right out and said it.

"Don't you two think, then, it is perhaps time to adopt me? I've always hoped you'd want to."

And that one remark by her, besides bringing more than any ordinary joy to both her foster parents, was the first step, because of its necessary legal actions that Kira took upon herself to manage and found interesting, the beginning of her decision to go to law school and become an attorney when college was over.

Seventeen

ana Weiss closed the file assembled by her husband's partner, Grace Garrity, on the Carleson girl, which he'd brought home, and looked across the coffee table at her husband.

"That's quite a report. Your Grace is turning out well." Dana put the file down on the coffee table. "Poor child. I mean the Carleson girl, not Grace. I have to feel sorry for her."

Alter Weiss bridled. "Cassandra Carleson? You have to be kidding."

"I'm not," Dana replied. "Yes, I know she's a spoiled-silly idle rich kid and all that, but I see someone else. She may have had an easy growing-up with a fancy home and dogs and horses and all, but she got punished endlessly by a stern unforgiving monster of a dad who sided against her with schools and everybody else. So, sorry, but I see a lost lonely kid always and one forever unjustly rebuked."

"You shrinks," Alter said accusingly and laughed. They were talking about how the billionaire Carleson's daughter, who had tossed a Molotov cocktail into a police car and assaulted a trooper, had got herself locked away two days ago in the city's notorious Weldon Prison while awaiting indictment and trial. It had seemed a shocking headline mystery to many. How could such a privileged young woman end up so badly?

Dana laughed at her husband. "Yes, I know, we apply psychology to everything. But haven't you wondered about Arthur Carleson recently suppressing an employee strike by simply shutting down a whole factory, leaving hundreds unemployed, most with wives and children to support? The guy's a monster, and ten to one he created a child who for all her activism has actually been expressing resistance to him and using the UWW to do so."

Detective Alter Weiss bowed, as he often did, to his psychologist wife's take on a suspect's motivation, her more often than not finding something good in someone whom he saw as basically bad. He'd been nailed by his superintendent to routinely check on the Carleson girl for any previous crimes. She'd been arrested in their precinct. So, feeling he was probably on a wild goose chase, Weiss took off that same day for Weldon.

Weiss hadn't known what to expect when, with Grace Garrity in tow and at the notorious prison, they were shown to a special interview room where prisoners thought to be dangerous could meet interrogating police or their lawyers.

Weiss was surprised by the girl who he found huddled on a chair at a table, hands and legs manacled, awaiting him in sullen silence. She was someone, he knew, who unless Father Andrew's confessional revelation was false, was not whom she herself and everyone else thought her to be.

Besides, she looked Baltic, he thought. She was strikingly pretty, with natural blond hair capping a face that seemed more the kind of face Weiss had seen often among many when he'd had to investigate crime in the Baltic Ghetto. It was the kind of face one usually thought of as Russian rather than American.

Asking routine questions about her part in the UWW, specifically where she had got the Molotov cocktail, had she made it herself or had she had help, and if help from whom, he heard only a sullen justification from a defiant and very angry young woman on how the police deserved it for protecting her guilty father, the principal object of the UWW activism.

When neither Weiss nor his partner got any answers to questions they asked the suspect, nor saw indication of any previous crimes, they finally gave up on the interview and left with the accused still huddled on her chair and muttering defiantly.

On the way out Weiss asked a guard if she's had a visit from her lawyer.

"Didn't have one until last night," the guard said. "You just missed the lady. She was here right before you. Big time. Came from Barasch and McGregor."

Weiss knew the name at once. It was a sprawling powerful law firm that didn't match with the defendant he's just interviewed and who normally would have got a court-appointed lawyer. How did the girl ever land with them?

"What was the lady's name?" he asked.

The guard glanced down at his log book. "Name's Danziger, Kira Danziger."

For a moment, time stood still for Weiss. Had he heard clearly? Was this the Kira he'd lost track of when tracing her through the welfare council, and had left her when she was placed in a second foster home? No, it couldn't be. He finally found his voice. "You said Kira? Kira Danziger. You're kidding."

"Not, sir. Brought her to the prisoner myself and checked her ID."

Before thanking the guard, Weiss stared blankly at him a moment, his thoughts a jumble. Kira the Carleson girl's lawyer? It just wasn't possible. Even though Kira was a rare name it had to be a different Kira.

Back in the police car, he snapped at Grace Garrity. "You missed one. Get on your tablet. City records, Kira Danziger. Check a possible name change."

A little startled by his obvious annoyance, his partner obeyed, and a few minutes later, when still not yet arrived at the police station, she got back to him, her tone sheepish.

"Yeah, sorry. Never thought to. Didn't think her name important. Kira Danziger changed her name some time s ago when adopted by foster parents. Before Kira Danziger, she was Kira Paulauskas."

Eighteen

The twenty-odd lawyers in the prestigious firm of Barasch and McGregor practiced everything from criminal to corporate law and from defense to prosecution. A small branch of several lawyers, each usually fresh out of law school, provided attorneys for those who could not afford a defense and who were paid not by earnings, which were minimal, but by the small charity attached to the firm by a foundation established by a wealthy philanthropist for just that purpose.

One of these young attorneys who had graduated top of her class at law school, and had been bid for by every law firm in the city, was Kira Danziger. Her brilliance had been successfully wooed by Barasch and McGregor, and in just short of a year she had handled four difficult cases, three of which she had won.

Ever gaining confidence in her new profession, Kira came to work one day to find that a case in which a young woman had torched the car of a state police trooper, and had assaulted the officer himself, had landed with the law firm, but nobody had yet been appointed attorney.

The moment she found out about the case and who the accused was, she edged two other young attorneys to one side in a firmly insistent request to be allowed to defend. With her request granted by the law firm's partners, she set to work at once.

Kira had felt an immediate emotional jolt when she'd heard the name of the accused. The years had rolled back and the memories had begun, first as shadowy long-forgotten hazy mental images of her mother in shabbily out-of-place clothes, kneeling to rake ashes from a fireplace, then memories of herself by her mother's side clutching a corner of her skirt, of strange people passing by without speaking as her mother scrubbed an oven, of herself looking at pictures in a book and frightened at her mother's absence elsewhere when she was put out of sight in a corner of some room—was it the kitchen? Of toying with the tablet, looking at games and cartoons when again put out of the way in the corner of another room.

And then of the Carleson child she was so often pulled roughly away from when she'd sneaked away from her mother to find a friendship with her in the nursery or the kitchen. And in her loneliness, and save for her mother an isolation from any others, her finding a solace in that friendship that sustained her until past the age of seven when her life became school and her joining Masha and the street gang.

Deciding she could not adequately defend Cassandra Carleson, nor even inform her that she was her attorney without knowing something of all Cassandra's years after she had ceased going to the Carleson home with her mother and, even though most of those years had been thoroughly exposed by the media, Kira set out to discover what changes there'd been in her childhood friend.

What indications were there, Kira wondered, as to the who her earliest childhood friend had become, which the press had skipped over with headlines like "Rich Kid" and "Dad Gets a Jab." What, if anything, could be found in her home and family that might help her defense?

Kira located a private phone for Orchards and made an appointment with a coldly guarded Miss Miller to see either Mrs. or Mr. Carleson there, rather than Mr. Carleson alone at his extensive offices downtown in the city. Driving herself to the sprawling country estate seemed almost like yesterday as her memory of it came back, and she was as impressed, as she had once been long ago, by the size and wealth of the big colonial mansion when only halfway up the winding gravel drive to it.

Her appearance at the door was met by a uniformed maid who showed her to a small office and a haughty ageing Miss Miller herself, whom she vaguely remembered as much younger, and who told her with the same remembered frostiness that Mr. Carleson would see her shortly, and then silently escorted her to the library where they would meet.

The pervasive memory of her mother's lowly cleaning, her difference and thus her own, was reinforced with the appearance after what seemed an interminably long wait, and with a haughtily protective Miss Miller present, of Arthur Carleson, whose cold disdain for her presence was also one of her memories.

Kira had done her homework on the man and was well prepared for his arrogance, and the interview proved short, less than ten minutes, with curt evasive answers to a few well prepared questions that revealed a nonexistent relationship between Carleson and his daughter, save for discipline.

But those ten minutes told Kira a lot about the young woman she would defend. Arthur Carleson, she realized, was as guilty as her client of torching the police vehicle and assaulting the trooper. Acutely aware of how her client must have developed a growing resistance to authority of any kind after years of protecting herself against someone who proved, even in a brief interview, to be as ruthlessly dominant as portrayed by the press, Kira saw why her client had become an aggressive activist. Even as a child, Cassandra Carleson had learned activism through what must have been the endless injustices of her father.

Driving away from Orchards, Kira saw the wealth surrounding Cassandra all her life as not in any way a benefit, but as a sort of golden prison where her client, through endless severity and suppression, had literally been trained to activism and violence. Would the ruthlessly cold bars of jail help lessen the lack of any sympathy for her childhood friend in the criminal court system? Kira could only hope it would.

Nineteen

Cassandra reluctantly aroused herself from fitful sleep on the bare bench of the holding cell where the only other amenities were a sink with a cold-water tap and a toilet without a seat.

"Get up. Your lawyer's waiting."

Lawyer? For a moment Cassandra didn't understand, but when she did, and with a sense of hopeless resignation, she rose and extended first both arms to be manacled again, then both legs attached to a waist chain. Pulled roughly upright, she was led slowly from the cell.

The interview room to which Cassandra was summarily taken was nearly as barren as the cell she'd left. There was a bare table and two chairs facing each other across it. At one, Cassandra was surprised to see who she'd been assigned as a lawyer. It was a smartly dressed and groomed dark-haired woman her own age, who sat in one of the chairs, looking though a file. When Cassandra was led by the guard to the other chair and unmanacled, the woman rose, and extending hand across the table between them, said, "Hi. I'm Kira Danziger, your lawyer."

The introductory moment meant nothing to Cassandra, who didn't even look up, but it meant quite a bit to Kira, who for the first time got a good look at the person she was assigned to defend and whose home she had only just been to. Even while making allowances for Cassandra having had little time to recover groomed looks since the riot, she was surprised by her degraded appearance, not so much by her lack of makeup and her tangled blond hair badly in need of a wash, but by the dark shadows under her eyes, her deathly pale color.

"We have to talk," Kira said. "You're facing a possible thirty years of your life thrown away in prison for tossing a Molotov cocktail into a police car and assaulting a trooper. I don't want that any more than I think you do. You've had a life leading up to it being provoked by years of facing unjust discipline from the son of a bitch you call father, and all the sycophants around him, like Miss Miller and schoolteachers and others. I'm going to build your case on that. On being raised from early childhood to protest injustice. So let's get off the defensive and talk."

Kira waited through a long silence, in which Cassandra straightened up when she'd heard her father cursed, but wouldn't look at her directly. She found herself once more wondering about Cassandra's very blond hair, when at Orchards she'd observed endless family photos and had been struck by the dark hair on all and by photographs of several ancestors as well who looked positively Mediterranean.

With Cassandra's hair being very blond, she'd compared a DNA sample taken by police in their investigation into whether Cassandra was a terrorist and a DNA sample she'd secretly taken herself from evidence of Arthur Carleson in the library at Orchards.

The two didn't match. A search into Rowena Carleson's possible adultery had brought her up short, however. The tabloids forever covering Rowena's being often seen with a reported lover, the blond film star Sven Nord, a Swede by birth, had reported Rowena to be living at home with Arthur at the conception time for Cassandra while the actor was in Japan making a film.

With the DNA samples being dissimilar, Kira felt plagued by a question. Was Cassandra then an adopted child? She had found no record of adoption at any time by the Carlesons. So, who then was the child she now faced in the prison interview room, and how had she become a Carleson? Kira was completely puzzled. The Cassandra Carleson she had long been identified as, and thought to be all of her life, was not the Cassandra of her birth certificate but somebody else. But who?

None of it made sense to Kira, and thinking she had to start somewhere to find out, she took a breath and said firmly, "Cassandra, look at me, please."

She had to say it twice before Cassandra finally did, and then Kira said, "I want you to do something for me. I want you to try to remember when you were very small. Like four and five and six, and especially seven."

"Remember?" It was the first word Cassandra had spoken, and Kira felt rewarded by it. She laughed slightly.

"Yes, remember," she said. "I know going back to that age is hard, but try. It's terribly important."

She paused, fixing Cassandra with a look. "Can you possibly remember a shabby old cleaning woman on her knees doing things like removing ashes from fireplaces, or scrubbing floors and cleaning ovens, and a little child your age staying close at her side and clutching the woman's apron?"

She stopped, and then reaching out and seizing one of Cassandra's hands, said, "Try to remember, please. You were, I'm sure, watching, and when you tried to talk to that child, remember being pulled away by Nanny or someone."

Kira took a deep breath and then said, "Cassandra, that child was me. Don't you remember, the tablet we played on? And the picture books when you found me stowed away in a corner someplace, and sneaked me into the nursery, and all the talking and giggling we shared looking at pictures until we got caught and separated again. And once sharing some cookies with Cook, who was the only one who didn't keep us apart and with whom we always felt safe. Don't you remember? Cassie, that she was me."

And Kira was finally rewarded by Cassandra suddenly reaching out and grabbing her other hand like one drowning, and saying, as tears came to her eyes, "Oh, my God. Oh, my God, yes. And I remember your name. Someone called you Kira. And being in my bedroom one time to look at TV and getting caught. You were yanked away like you were about to kill me or had a terrible disease or something, and I got punished for talking to you at all. Oh, my God, yes, Kira. So many things whenever you came. And that's you here now? You? Kira, I can't believe this. All those years ago? Oh, Kira."

Twenty

In the busy police station, the telephone on Detective Alter Weiss's desk rang. He picked up the receiver and said, "Yes?"

"Detective Weiss?"

"Speaking."

"This is Kira Danziger. I'm the attorney for Cassandra Carleson, the woman who torched the police car."

Caught off guard a moment by her returning call, his name was all he could say as he struggled to reconcile the Kira Danziger he'd slowly learned about with the reality of her voice on the phone, and then with the impossibility of her being the defending attorney for the child she'd been exchanged with when a baby. It was unreal and made no sense at all. Kira Danziger was an impersonal woman he'd tracked up through her years like one of his many police cases. Kira Danziger was someone swapped for another by a cleaning-woman mother soon after her birth and whom he'd given up on when she was placed in a second foster home. She was only real as part of an investigation.

He heard her voice again. She was saying, "I need to meet with you and go through some information I have that has to do with your partner's investigation of Miss Carleson's life, which over the years I believe has been quite extensive."

One thought only immediately began to race through Weiss's mind. Grace Garrity had somehow let things get out of hand. In an immediate mixture of anger at Grace and curiosity as to how much of her investigation his partner had revealed, he again heard the attorney say that she hoped to build enough of a case for Cassandra, "to get the DA's demand for thirty years in prison reduced to perhaps no more than three, with some time on probation. Impossible, I know," she said, "but I plan to do it." And then ask again, insistently, if they could meet, and where it would be convenient for him. "I might need you as a possible witness."

Weiss couldn't see how the child he'd tracked up through her years had any possible connection to the one who'd attacked the police, but pulling himself together, and starting finally to think sensibly, he said, "Of course, Miss Danziger."

The attorney clearly knew something of his investigation into her life as Kira Paulauskas, as well as Grace's investigation into Cassandra Carleson's. The question was what bearing did one have on the other. It might be wise, he thought, to have his always clearheaded psychologist wife present. What her reaction would be to Kira Danziger being a reality, he could only imagine.

He stalled. "I have a heavy day. Would you mind meeting me at my home this evening?"

Kira said that was fine by her, and after setting a time with him, hung up, leaving Weiss thoroughly disturbed by a whole jumble of unanswered questions.

He managed to finished work early, went home, got his children busy with homework, and briefed his wife.

"I couldn't believe it when she said she was Cassandra's attorney," he told Dana. "How is it possible?"

"Maybe not as strange as you might think, Alt." Dana seemed astonishingly unflustered, as though Kira Danziger appearing in their lives was the most natural thing in the world. She said, "We may be a city, Alt, but we're not New York or Chicago, and somehow a relatively small town when it comes to some things. Second-rate lawyers abound, of course. But there are only two law firms the Carleson girl would have landed in a case this big, courtesy probably of the UWW. Not when she graduated law school with honors. Your Kira would hardly have accepted representation by Philby, Earnst and Holt either. They're her father's lawyers. So she went to their fiercest competitor. Barasch and McGregor. Okay for that, but what's she using for money? Is the UWW paying for her attorney? I doubt it, and she's been disowned, according to the press, and living on her own."

"Barasch and McGregor," Weiss said, "often provides legal aid to those who can't afford it. Helps polish their public image. We use them occasionally in my department."

They had hardly finished talking and trying to imagine what Kira Danziger would ask them and planning responses that might seem adequate when their doorbell rang and Dana answered it to admit the attorney, and both she and her husband found themselves looking at a young smartly dressed woman wearing a designer tailored suit, her well-groomed dark hair partially held back on one side with a gold clip and carrying what Dana recognized at once as an Hermès handbag.

She introduced herself with poised courtesy itself, apologizing for an evening meeting, and after being served coffee by Dana, got down to business almost immediately.

"Detective Weiss," she said, first addressing Alter. "You've been conducting an extensive investigation of my client. And please don't say it's because of Cassandra torching the police vehicle. It began long before that. You have also been investigating me right back to me in sixth grade and possibly earlier."

For a second time that day, Weiss found himself

more than uncomfortable that she had learned of his investigation as separate from Grace's. How could he have been so unaware?

Her answer didn't help; in fact it threw him completely. "But let's for the moment," she said, "skip over your partner's extensive discoveries starting long before Cassandra's college days and activism. Let's instead talk instead about me, Kira, when I was Kira Paulauskas, before my name change. My life. How much of it do you know? I think you first came across me, perhaps, when I was ten and I ran away from home when my mother, Emilija, died and I got picked up by cops and handed over to welfare. Am I right?"

Weiss found himself looking at a person who was all attorney, and who smiled pleasantly, but not with her eyes. Her eyes stared back at him with a steady look of determination that dared any challenge. Evasion wouldn't work with this young woman, whom he was actually seeing for the first time in reality and no longer as a homeless ten-year-old from the Baltic Ghetto.

Caught out, Weiss knew he was going to have to answer any questions she had. But first, he had a question of his own. It was, "Miss Danziger, why is whatever I may know about your life relevant to the case of arson against Miss Carleson?"

"Fair enough," Kira answered. "In my building a real defense for Cassandra, you ought to first know it's not due to some quirk of fate or some other aberration that I represent her. I chose to,

Detective Weiss. And I did so because I knew Cassandra early in childhood when my mother was obliged to drag me along on cleaning jobs at the Carleson home. You saw in your investigation of me what Cassandra's life was like in its first seven years. Your partner's report goes into all the beginnings of a defenseless daughter being treated unjustly by a ruthlessly dominant father. Which then dragged on for years and was a prime factor in her becoming an activist."

Looking steadily back at her and taking in her expensive suit and her careful grooming, Weiss was sure her long road up out of darkness hadn't been due to good luck but to her own determination to have a higher standing in life than Emilija's, and realizing the only person who could ever get it for her was herself.

Adding up all he'd learned about her, however, he knew that her life as well as her client's was missing one factor. That was the truth about themselves, who they both actually were. Kira Danziger, especially, deserved, he thought, not to go into a courtroom without the evidence that could be decisive in a defense of her client. She needed to complete the picture that was the lives of both her and Cassandra, and he was the only one who could provide the evidence that would let her do it.

He said, "Fair enough," and turned from Kira to his wife, knowing almost immediately that she felt as he did, that they had to reveal all they actually knew. *Why resist* was written all over Dana's face:

that Cassandra Carleson would find out somehow but needed to know, not someday because of her own perseverance, but right now with the whole future life of one of the babies swapped at risk.

Weiss spread his hands in surrender and said, "All right, Miss Danziger. I think there's something you ought to see, if you'll give me just a moment."

He rose and went to the safe in the next room, spun the dial, and moments later came back with the two folded pages of Father Andrew's revelation of the confession by Emilija Paulauskas.

He said, "This was given to me in utter confidence which my wife and I have always honored. I hope in giving it to you to read, we can trust in yours and your client's confidence also."

He didn't ask for an answer or any promises. He knew the woman to whom he was giving Father Andrew's extraordinary revelation, and there was a long silence while Kira read and Weiss and his wife waited.

Twenty-One

When Kira finished reading, and after a moment of staring silently off into space, she said quietly, to herself, "But, of course. The blond hair. But how could I have ever guessed?"

And then, looking up from the letter at the silently waiting detective and his wife, both clearly expecting her to be shocked, Kira found herself instead almost amused and silently wondering how you explained to anyone your not being surprised at all by such a revelation when it simply makes clear why a bond formed years ago in childhood had finally come full circle. The confession by Cassandra's real mother of her sad and tortured exchange of two infants is really just confirmation as to why life for Cassandra and her became what it was and they the people they were.

When she returned Father Andrew's letter to a silent Weiss, Kira said calmly, and with a smile, "Thank you for your interest in all this, Detective Weiss. You've been something of a guardian angel for me, at least in your interest in my being alone as a ten-year-old until I became Kira Danziger. But put it back in your safe, or better still, destroy it if you feel giving it to me betrays Father Andrew's confidence in your strict secrecy."

She laughed slightly in adding, "Up to you, but I agree it will certainly be critical in court to my defense of Cassandra. Other than that, I don't think that it's of any real importance that I was once briefly Cassandra, nor she once Kira Paulauskas, and that our very different lives once began as other people. She and I are who we've become, not who our names or any birthright identifies us as." Kira shrugged dismissively. "And I suspect that Cassandra will agree. Neither she nor I can turn the clock back, to put things right."

Looking at a silent Weiss, she saw affirmed in his whole manner his understanding and acknowledged agreement with what she'd said, while his wife broke the silence with a single word, "Amen."

"So, even though a late hour," Kira said, "let's at least get started on planning a court strategy, shall we? One that will find the revelation of the actual birthright for my client a reason for her starting down a different path in life entirely, with a guide, no matter how slight, her early childhood memory of the desperately poor old cleaning woman who was her real mother, who had placed her in a life of wealth in an exchange with another. And to know, also, that the other child in that exchange will always be there for her."

Epilogue

On a softly warm spring day, and as the bell high in the tower of the church of St. Mary Magdelene rang the hour, two young women were seen amidst the timeworn gravestones of the church's old cemetery. One, her manacled hands clutching flowers, was followed discreetly by a police officer.

They stopped by one gravestone that was newer than any of the others, and while the manacled woman knelt in prayer after laying flowers on the grave, the other stood in silence, her head bowed, her hands clasped over her heart.

After a while, with her companion's arm protectively around her shoulders, the manacled woman rose and the two left the graveyard and the gravestone on which was simply inscribed only the name EMILIJA PAULAUSKAS, along with the dates of her birth and death.

About the Author

David Osborn, for over sixty years a writer, lives in Connecticut with his wife, a once American and European ballerina, then renowned in international health policy. Their daughter, a PhD psychologist, practices in Sydney, Australia. Their lawyer son is an advocate for the welfare of animals worldwide.

Also by David Osborn

Novels and Screenwriting

Novels

The Glass Tower – Hodder & Stoughton

Open Season – The Dial Press

The French Decision – Doubleday

Love and Treason – New American Library

Heads – Bantam

Murder on Martha's Vineyard – Lynx

Murder on the Chesapeake – Simon & Schuster

Murder in the Napa Valley – Simon & Schuster

The Last Pope – Source Books

The Cape Cod Blue – Dagmar Miura

Alicia's Secret (young adult) – Dagmar Miura

A Cold Wind from the Andes – Dagmar Miura

The Head Hunters – Dagmar Miura

Looking Back: The Long Life of a Writer (a memoir)

Delta Red – Dagmar Miura

Eventide – Dagmar Miura

The Somersville Bodies – Dagmar Miura

Cold Case 369 – Dagmar Miura

The Lighthouse (a novella)– Dagmar Miura

The Saugatuck Conspiracy – Dagmar Miura

Bones – Dagmar Miura

Kira and Cassandra – Dagmar Miura

For Children

Jessica and the Crocodile Knight (a novel) – HarperCollins

Jessica and Her Adventures in Fairyland (collection of five novellas) – Dagmar Miura

Ophelia and Her Forest Friends (series of ten stories) – Dagmar Miura

Jessica and the Witch's Broom – Dagmar Miura

Jessica and the Flying Unicorns – Dagmar Miura

Jessica and the Golden Swan Feather – Dagmar Miura

Feature Films

The Trap (original story and screenplay; Academy Award nominee for Best Foreign Film) – Columbia

Open Season (screenplay, adapted from Osborn's own best-selling novel *Open Season*) – Columbia

Chase a Crooked Shadow (original story and screenplay co-written with Charles Sinclair; listed by the British Academy of Motion Picture Science as "One of the ten best suspense scripts ever written") – Warner Bros.

Moment of Danger, a.k.a. *Malaga* (screenplay adapted from the novel) – Warner Bros.

Malaga (screenplay) – Warner Bros.

Maroc 7 (original story and screenplay) – J. Arthur Rank

Deadlier Than the Male (original story and screenplay) – J. Arthur Rank

Some Girls Do (original story and screenplay) – J. Arthur Rank

The Road to Dusty Death (screenplay) – J. Arthur Rank

The Games (screenplay) – Associated British

Follow the Boys (original story and screenplay) – MGM

Beat Girl (original story and screenplay) – Renown Films/British Lion

Stop-over Forever (original story and screenplay) – British Lion

Winter Holiday (original story and screenplay) – MGM

Penny Gold (original story and screenplay) – J. Arthur Rank/Columbia

Whoever Slew Auntie Roo? (original story and screenplay) – Paramount & American International

Murder, She Said (screenplay, Agatha Christie adaptation) – MGM

Murder at the Gallop (screenplay, Agatha Christie adaptation) – MGM

Feature-Length Documentaries

Fangio, The History of Formula One Racing (original screenplay; executive producer) – Volpi Productions

Why Ireland – Irish Tourist Bureau

Films Canceled While in Production

HMS Ulysses – Volpi Productions (screenplay adaptation of the Alistair MacLean novel about protecting North Sea convoys to Russia during World War II; production halted when a key warship was unavailable)

The Mad Motorists – Volpi Productions (screenplay adaptation from the Allen Andrews novel about the 1907 Peking to Paris race)

Eagle at Sundown – Dragon Films (original screen story about Napoleon's escape from Elba; starring Douglas Fairbanks; in production when canceled)

Les Petits Rats – Disney (original story and screenplay about the Paris Ballet school; production begun, then canceled)

Hunters' Horn – McCahon Productions (screenplay adaptation from the Harriette Simpson Arnow novel; production canceled; financing failure)

Blood on the Rose – British Lion (screenplay adaptation from the Phyllis Hastings novel)

Television

Bouquet for Miss Olive (three-act play; British Television Producers Association nominee for Best Play of the Year) – Granada/ITV

Three on a Gas Ring (three-act play; British Television Producers Association nominee for Best Play of the Year) – Granada/ITV

Why George Brown Hanged (three-act play) – Granada/ITV

Arthur of the Britons (pilot and three scripts on the life of King Arthur; Writers Guild of Great Britain award winner for Best British Children's Series)

The Antiquers (original story, pilot, and six episodes in the sitcom series) – Irish National Television